The Heart of Home

OTHER BOOKS BY STEPHENIA H. MCGEE

Ironwood Plantation
The Whistle Walk
Heir of Hope
Missing Mercy
*Ironwood Series Set
*Get the entire series at a discounted price

The Accidental Spy Series
*Previously published as The Liberator Series
An Accidental Spy
A Dangerous Performance
A Daring Pursuit
*Accidental Spy Series Set
*Get the entire series at a discounted price

Stand Alone Titles
In His Eyes
Eternity Between Us

Time Travel
Her Place in Time
(Stand alone, but ties to Rosswood from The Accidental Spy Series)
The Hope of Christmas Past
(Stand alone, but ties to Belmont from In His Eyes)

Novellas
The Heart of Home
The Hope of Christmas Past

www.StepheniaMcGee.com
Sign up for my newsletter to be the first to see new cover reveals
and be notified of release dates
New newsletter subscribers receive a free book!
Get yours here
bookhip.com/QCZVKZ

The Heart of Home

STEPHENIA H. MCGEE

"When thou passest through the waters, I will be with thee; and through the rivers, they shall not overflow thee…"

Isaiah 42:2a

Chapter One

Riverbend Plantation
Greenville, Mississippi
August, 1865

The pesky tribulations of life always seemed more stifling in the wake of departing company. Opal Martin watched her friend's carriage roll away and continued to stare down the curve of the drive long after the dust settled. The trees rustled in the breeze as though they thought to wave as well, but merely shuddered instead. She let her hand linger on the knob a moment longer, and then let herself back into the empty foyer.

She should be used to the sparseness by now. They'd gone for years without the finery that had once graced this pride of Daddy's legacy. Now the big house of Riverbend was little more than leftovers scraped from the Yankees' fine china.

Closing the door to keep out the bugs even though it smothered the breeze, Opal tried not to think of the summers they had once spent in Virginia or abroad to avoid the heat and the mosquitoes. At least she and

Mama didn't have to bear the unpleasantness of August alone. Others spent their summers here as well, most notably her dear friends and neighbors Westley and Ella Remington.

Ella had been kind to bring the baby by, his childish giggles offering a few moments of glee that tended to shoo out the loneliness. Mama coveted their company, even if she acted like guests were a burden. The light in her faded eyes glimmered more when baby Lee came by than at any other time.

With a practiced glide of yellow skirts over the freshly swept floors, Opal returned to the monotony of living in an empty plantation in war-ravished lands. She found Mama in the parlor, tidying up. They kept most of their furnishings here, by way of having at least one space that felt somewhat normal. The settee didn't match the chairs, and the worn green carpet almost clashed with the pale blue curtains. But she wouldn't complain. Nearly half of these things were gifts from the Remingtons and had not been easy to come by. They had plenty to be thankful for.

Mama's black cotton skirts shifted in the paltry breeze allowed through the lace curtains of the parlor window. "I remember a time when a lady never had to dirty her hands with cleaning up after company," she grumbled, plucking two shortbreads from the plate and wrapping them in a napkin for later.

And there had been a time when Mama wouldn't have thought to save uneaten tea refreshments, but those days were long gone. "It was nice of them to come and visit."

2

"Don't see why they do. They have plenty up at Belmont. Why lower themselves to the likes of Riverbend?"

Opal stacked the teacups on the tray and settled it against her hip. "Ella is my dear friend, Mama. She comes for the company."

Mama grunted something, but Opal didn't stick around to see what it would be this time. No doubt Mama merely voiced a variation of one of the complaints Opal had heard dozens of times. A knock sounded at the door, causing her to turn from her trek to the kitchen.

Had Ella returned already? She balanced the tray on her hip once again and opened the door. A bespectacled man with a fine linen suit and a fashionable cap slung low over his sandy hair gave a small bow.

"Good afternoon, Miss."

Opal narrowed her eyes and looked past him. Where had he come from unnoticed?

The man followed her gaze. "My horse threw a shoe up the road."

"That so?"

He doffed the hat and put it under his arm, offering a smile as slick as his oiled hair. "Yes. Mind if I come in?"

She tightened her grip on the door. "Surely you saw the carriage, then?"

"No," he said, looking over her shoulder and into the house. "Didn't see a carriage."

Had the man actually left his horse at the road—an incredibly foolish thing, as it would likely not be there upon his return—then he couldn't have possibly missed Ella's carriage as she left the drive and he entered it.

Opal stepped back and made to close the door. "I'm sorry, sir. You'll have to seek aid elsewhere."

"Wait!" He thrust out a hand.

She hesitated, looking over her shoulder. Where had Mama gone?

"Forgive me. I don't mean to frighten you." He took a step back. "I aim to help you."

"Help me?" Her brow furrowed. "Didn't you just say you needed help yourself?"

The man smiled again and straightened, giving Opal an appraising glance. She set her teeth, both offended and self-conscious. Her dress had long since become threadbare, and though Ella had insisted on giving her new cloth, her lack of skill in sewing had thus far concocted only one half-finished skirt. She ran a hand down the fabric. "Sir, I must bid you good day."

"You'll not hear my offer?" He sucked a quick breath, not bothering to wait for her response. "I've come looking for a fine piece of property to purchase, and as I happened upon yours, it caught my fancy."

"Our home is not for sale. Good day to you."

Opal closed the door on his sputtering and made sure the lock slid into place. She'd heard tell of Northern opportunists seeking to take advantage of the misfortunes of the South, but had not expected to find one upon her doorstep! What would a dandy like that know of planting crops?

She carried the tray through the house and out to the kitchen, where she found Mama scrutinizing a bag of flour. "Do you suppose we will have enough to make a pie?"

Opal set the tray down, hoping Mama wouldn't notice it wobbled.

Mama shook the flour sack, then her head, answering her own question. "What took you so long?" She shot Opal a sidelong glance, her eyes narrowing in on the rattle of the teakettle.

"There was a stranger at the door." Opal set the cups aside and wiped crumbs from the tray with a tattered rag.

Mama dropped the flour on the table, sending up a puff of white dust. "A stranger?"

"Yes. Said he had a horse throw a shoe at the road and came for help."

She smacked her hands together, and then snagged the rag to remove the last traces from her thin fingers. "Then he should have come across Mrs. Remington."

"Um-hum." Opal pried open the saltbox. Only two slabs of ham remained within. "I said the same, but he claimed not to have seen the carriage. He wanted to come in the house, but I refused him."

Mama peered over Opal's shoulder, and the force of her dramatic sigh stirred Opal's hair. "We certainly don't need any vagrants trying to take up shelter here."

The fellow had been dressed far too fine to be a vagrant, but there would be no reason to tell Mama that. They would never sell their home to a Northerner anyhow.

They tidied up the kitchen in companionable silence, and when the chores were finished, Opal sliced the last of this morning's bread while Mama set out a new loaf to rise. Wiping the pricks of sweat from her forehead, she laid the slices on the tray and plucked one of the slabs of ham from the saltbox. Her nose crinkled at the thought of another meal of salt pork, but at least they were not going without. Ella's gift of blackberry jam would sweeten it nicely.

Mama eyed the tray Opal assembled and pressed her lips into a line. The expression only made her look all the more pinched. Opal's heart ached. Daddy's death had taken too much of a toll on Mama. Perhaps she could have endured the rest of the hardships, had she the reassurance that Daddy would return to them. Mama passed through the door, leaving Opal to secure everything for the evening.

They'd discovered a vacant-eyed man dressed in Confederate rags rummaging through their supplies two weeks ago. Opal sent him on his way with a loaf of bread and a pouch of pecans, but ever since then they'd locked the kitchen up tight well before sunset.

Opal hummed softly to herself as she made her way back through the house, setting the tray down on the dining table that had blessedly been too much for the soldiers to carry off.

She picked up the jam to begin readying their meal when a strange noise slid through the open window and drew her attention. Opal paused. Had that carpetbagger returned? She plunked the jam down on the table and strode through the house, pulling open the front door, only to find the porch empty. She stuck her head out and scanned the wide expanse of the porch, at least as far as she could see in either direction before it wrapped around the house, and then looked out across the yard. No sign of anyone. The hairs on the back of her neck stood on end.

"What's going on?" Mama's voice, tight with worry, pricked Opal's ears.

Opal forced her shoulders to relax. "It's nothing, Mama, I just heard a noise."

A low growl issued from the side of the house, the warning the mongrel that hung around usually gave whenever someone came to call. Mama must have heard it too, because she pushed past Opal onto the porch.

"Hello? Who's there?"

"Mama!" Opal grabbed Mama's arm. "What if it's someone of ill intent?"

Mama waved her hand. "The war is over."

As though that did a lick of good these days. It wasn't the soldiers they had to worry about as much as the lawless miscreants who went about harassing good folks. Opal shivered. Why, they may as well have gone west out to the untamed frontier for as much as society had stayed intact.

Opal gave Mama's arm a tug. "Don't you remember the fellow we found in the kitchen?"

"Precisely. We haven't the means to lose our goods to another one." Opal opened her mouth to retort, but Mama held up a hand. "And before you say it, I do not want to continue to beg from the Remingtons. Our debt to them has grown far too deep."

At the moment, this wasn't an argument to rehash. "Then let us not stand out on the porch as easy targets."

She tugged Mama's sleeve. "Let's lock ourselves inside."

A rustling turned the dog's growl to a ferocious barking. Then it gave a sharp whimper and came running around the corner of the house, scurrying up the steps to cower behind Opal.

Frowning, she reached down to remove her skirts from his muddy fur and his wide tongue slathered the back of her hand. She grimaced and instinctively wiped her hand down the fabric, further sullying it.

"Oh, hello there!"

Oh, no. The too-friendly voice disgusted her almost as much as the dog's lick. She almost hated to look up, knowing who she would see. A wide smile stretched across the face of the man she had already dismissed from their land as he stepped onto the lowest porch stair. She flexed her fingers into her dress and moved around Mama, who merely stood there blinking rapidly. "Sir, what are you doing lurking about our home?"

"Why, I already told you, miss. I'm considering buying it." He hooked his thumbs into his lapels and rocked back on his heels, his gaze traveling up the front columns. "A man should get a good look before making an investment, you see."

Mama made a funny sound in her throat and turned to Opal. "What's this?"

Opal leveled the stranger with a flat stare, answering Mama even as she didn't take her gaze from the man. "This is the stranger who wanted to come into the house. I told you about him earlier."

Tossing her head, Mama smoothed her dress and clasped her hands as though she was entertaining company. "You said nothing about a fine gentleman interested in the house."

Opal swung her gaze from the grin on the man's face to Mama's assessing gaze. Had she gone mad? "That is because it is utter foolishness. The house is not for sale."

"Allow me to introduce myself," the man said, bending at the waist. "I am Mr. Donald Weir."

"And what brings you to Riverbend, Mr. Weir?" Mama asked politely, her Southern charms as easily donned as a familiar shawl.

Opal bit back a seething retort begging for release. Surely Mama could see precisely what kind of man stood before them and his intentions couldn't be more obvious. He aimed to take advantage of two lone women hanging onto the ragged hem of war.

"I was passing through the area when I noticed what a fine home you have here on the river. I simply had to come and see it."

"I thought you said your horse threw a shoe." Opal truly *tried* to keep the derision from her voice, but the caustic burn of Mama's glare indicated she'd failed.

The side of his mouth twitched. "It did. I left it tied at the road."

Mama lifted her brows. "I fear that was an unwise action, Mr. Weir. Good horses are in scant supply, and you may not find it where you left it."

He blinked as though such a thing had never occurred to him, and Opal had to wonder if the fellow was equal parts liar and fool.

"Perhaps I should retrieve him." He glanced back

toward the road. "But could I come back later to discuss my thoughts on the house with you?"

"Why, I see no reason…" Opal began, but Mama stepped in front of her.

"You may, sir." She jabbed her elbow into Opal's arm.

"Thank you. Much obliged." He gave another bow and turned on his heel, striding away as though he'd just won some great victory.

Opal turned to Mama with a scowl. "What are you doing?"

"Do not speak to me with such disrespect, child," Mama said with a sniff. "I have my reasons."

She tried not to grind her teeth. "And what reasons could you possibly have for tolerating a man who clearly tried to hide his horse and sneak around our home undetected?"

"You have eyes." Mama lowered her voice, though the man was now out of hearing distance. "You can surely see the man is in a far better condition than the rest of us. Why, even Westley Remington hasn't been as finely dressed as that." She snagged a stray graying lock and pushed it back into the coil on the top of her head. "Mr. Weir may be an answer to prayer. Just what we need."

Opal crossed her arms. Why bring their friends into this? Mr. Remington's connections with the occupying army had kept them from starving. "We have no need of the likes of him."

Mama released a heavy breath. "You are growing too thin. Your cheeks are sinking in."

Taken aback, Opal dropped her arms and stared at Mama. What did her looks have to do with anything?

"The life we had is gone." Mama's shoulders sagged, and she appeared older beneath her widow's blacks. "Perhaps…." She lowered her eyes and fiddled with the cuff on her sleeve. "Perhaps it is time we start thinking of a new beginning."

Opal's heart somersaulted. A new beginning? As in leaving their home? She watched the stranger depart, Mama standing stiffly at her side. Opal studied the lines of Mama's profile. Had the losses settled so heavily upon her that she could no longer bear the home Daddy had built for her? Once these columns had felt like stately guardians. Did they now feel like prison bars?

Voice too tight for argument, Opal extracted her arm from Mama's grasp and turned to go back into the house, feeling nearly as empty as the vacant halls.

Chapter Two

Tristan Stuart's boots crunched along the river road, the toe of the left one flapping each time he took a step. He watched it with contempt as he continued the arduous trudge he'd thought would eventually take him back home. But that home no longer existed.

Mosquitoes buzzed around his face, drawn to the trickle of blood ever oozing from his hairline. He no longer bothered swatting them. They feasted upon him, but he couldn't bring himself to care. The news in Greenville had shattered his last remaining hope. What did more insect bites matter? His fingers itched to touch the five black bands tied around his arm, a steady reminder of his loss.

He scanned the trees lining one side of the road, and then shielded his eyes against the glimmer of the river on the other. The Mississippi churned, tinted brown with the sediment that would enrich the fields when the banks overflowed. He'd passed plenty of fields thus far, some charred black, others actually being tended. Either way, it didn't really matter. The river cared nothing for the woes of men. In some ways, the river was like life. It gave and took of its own volition, with no sense of justice. A mindless, violent force which could bless and curse in equal measure. It would continue its cycle, regardless of whether it lent aid to struggling farmers or destroyed them.

Tristan passed by one particularly green field, flanked by a large, red brick house. Scores of people moved about their work almost joyously, singing hymns as they swung hoes among the tender plants. Tristan didn't look long upon them.

He had no desire ever to farm again, let alone utter a hymn.

At least these people had found some joy in this battered place, ripe with their new freedoms. He wouldn't begrudge them their pointless singing. He placed one foot in front of the other, the heat bringing sweat down his forehead to mingle with the blood. Both dripped into his eyes. He blinked it away as he turned off the road and meandered up the bank of the river, not entirely sure where he thought to go. A man could find freedom in aimless wandering, even if that freedom only meant he no longer had to heed marching orders and could stop to watch the river if he chose.

The water glistened below, a tumult of muddy chaos. His eyes danced across the surface, watching as a stray leaf was caught up in the current and swirled away, only to be drawn into the depths as its reward for the ride.

Such had been his own tale. Swept into tides of war, only to find himself crushed beneath the choking waters of loss. He moved closer, allowing his feet to sink into the cool mud. The water lapped at his boots, urging him to come farther into comfort. He could be like the leaf, washed away into the blissful abyss that carried none of the raw angst chafing his soul.

He took another step into the river, the water now pulling at his knees. It would be easy to float away here. To let the river take him where it would. Another step and it tugged at his waist, a cold and wet embrace. Tristan ran his fingers through the water, letting it caress the dirt from his palms.

The sun sank lower, turning the sky a fiery orange that glimmered on the surface of the water. Another step and it took hold of his chest, nudging him farther. Another step, and it lifted his feet from underneath him. Tristan leaned back and let it sweep him into its arms, carrying him past the banks. He lay on his back, looking up at the changing sky. This felt far better than walking. How many miles had he walked in his four years with the army? Countless.

His body twisted and turned, spinning the sky around. Somewhere in the far reaches of his mind a forgotten worry niggled him, but he couldn't bring himself to pluck it free and examine it. What did it matter anyway? The river's embrace squeezed him tighter, pushing the air from his lungs. He drew another breath and spread his arms, trying to gain some balance as the current increased.

The water heaved, spinning him onto his stomach and sucking him beneath the surface. A long forgotten panic surged, and Tristan kicked his feet, fighting for the surface. Cold water wrapped around him, seeking to find its way into his nose and mouth. He kicked harder, frantically searching for the surface.

His fingers splayed, and in a moment of clarity, he realized he did not want to be the leaf swallowed by the abyss. Using a burst of energy he didn't think he possessed, Tristan reached for the surface and thrust his arms down at his sides, kicking with all of his might.

He broke free of the tendrils pulling at him and sucked a breath of air before the water pulled him under again. Struggling to break free, he battled the river around a hard bend, desperately trying to keep surfaced while fighting for land.

Finally, his fingers sank into thick mud and he clawed at it, heaving himself onto the bank. He flipped over onto his back, gulping in a lungful of humid air. The wind tickled across his brow. He stared up at the sky, loathing himself for being too cowardly to let the river take him to be reunited with his family.

Tristan slipped a finger under his jacket and touched the lowest band on his arm, the one meant for Millie. Then he closed his eyes and curled onto his side.

Tristan awoke with a start. A grunt had him scrambling for his rifle, forgetting it had been stolen from him somewhere outside of Tupelo. He rolled to his knees, his eyes darting around in the gathering gray of evening. The noise came again, a groaning that didn't seem human.

He scanned the bank, his eyes landing on a clump

of fur under a scraggly bush. He sat back on his haunches. The fur wiggled first, and then the rest of a dog scampered out from under the scrub brush, its coat a matted mess of mud. Tristan watched it as it slunk toward him. He didn't move, transfixed as the creature made its way to him and then rolled over, exposing a dirty belly.

Tristan shifted his eyes from the thrashing tail and up to a brown eye that seemed both welcoming and soulful. The dog turned on its side and scooted itself closer, bumping up against Tristan's boot before flipping over once again. He slowly reached out a hand, and the dog greeted him with a warm tongue. Despite himself, an unfamiliar smile pulled at the side of his mouth and he reached down to scratch behind the filthy fellow's ear. The dog nudged his hand, and in a moment, Tristan was sitting on the muddy bank rubbing the exuberant dog's belly.

Then without warning the dog flipped to his feet and pointed his nose down the bank, floppy ears held erect. Tristan followed the dog's gaze up to a large white house, its stately columns standing sentry against the coming night like a row of soldiers. They wrapped all the way around the house, and the sight of them made his stomach drop to his feet.

Willowby.

He blinked, but the vision didn't retreat. He looked down at the dog, and understanding dawned. At long last he would be granted a mercy. Light flickered in the window, beckoning him. Slowly, Tristan gained his feet and stumbled forward, trying to clear the fog from his mind. The pain in his head flared, and he didn't need to reach up to touch it to know the blood flowed once more.

The dog looked up at him and whimpered, and then scampered forward, looking over its shoulder. Tristan gave a nod. He would come. Perhaps his body had been taken down by the river after all. The dog merely guided him home, to the place where he would see them all once more.

He tried to swallow, his throat dry despite all the water he'd swallowed. He placed one foot in front of the other, feeling far too wearisome to be free of the confines of flesh. But then, what would he know of such things? Perhaps this was just the way of it. The house grew larger upon his approach, beckoning him to the quiet rest that would rid him of this troubled world.

He took the steps gingerly, reverently putting his hand on the column. The windows didn't look like he remembered them, and the river snaking through the rear yard wasn't true, but he wouldn't begrudge the changes in the vision. At least he had been granted a glimpse of home before his soul gave up its confinement. It was a far sight better than the churning waters of the Mississippi.

He sank onto the porch, and the dog settled by his side, snout resting on its paws. Tristan laid back, the faint sound of the door opening bringing peace. They would take him now, and he would drift away to where the streets were golden and pain did not rule. He'd lost sight of God during the swarms of battle, but as peace settled on his spirit, he knew God had not forgotten him.

Closing his eyes, Tristan waited for the bright light. *Forgive me for forgetting you, and remember me instead as the boy who once trusted you with his heart.*

"Who are you?"

The voice was smooth and soft, yet held more bite than an angel's should have.

"Naught but a weary soldier ready to go home."

A rustling of fabric and then the voice came closer. "Best you get on about that, then."

Exhaustion pulled at him, tugging him toward the comforts of oblivion. He nodded, the pulse in his head beating a steady rhythm with his somnolent heart. He was trying to get on with it. Couldn't the angel see that?

The sweet scent of honey tickled his nose and he sighed. Heaven would be a blessed reprieve from the fetid assault scores of wounded and unwashed men had waged on his senses.

The disgruntled voice softened and neared. "Um, are you all right, sir?"

He fought back a surge of irritation. Of course he wasn't all right. Was a dying man supposed to be? "Will be, soon as this is done."

"As soon as *what's* done?"

Tristan cracked an eye to examine the angel standing over him. Hair the color of warm coffee piled on top of her head, she stared at him with wide brown eyes from an oval face. He smiled. Just as beautiful as a heavenly creature should be. She leaned near and placed a cool hand on his brow, making a tsking sound as her fingers slid into what must be the matted mess of blood tangled in his hairline.

Pain spiked and he snagged her wrist, startled to find it all too solid in his grasp. His eyes flew wide. The woman should have struggled to get away, but she remained still, looking down at him with guarded eyes.

"Sir, you need tending."

Tristan swallowed, trying to get his foggy thoughts to focus. Was he dreaming? Or perhaps he was actually drowning in the river and his mind merely conjured a more pleasant place to pass. He released her hand. "Just let me be."

Scowling, she leaned closer. "You are on my porch."

Tristan groaned, the throbbing in his head trying to convince him this was not the quiet escape back to Willowby he'd yearned for.

"Sir?" She shook his shoulder, sending another wave of pain through his head.

He released a low groan and closed his eyes. "Just let me be, woman, I beg of you."

She scoffed. "I cannot. You are a drenched and delirious soldier still clothed in his grays and lying on my porch in a most pitiful state. I simply cannot *let you be.*"

Anger stirred in his chest, pushing out some of the cold from his veins. The dog at his side moved closer, its warm body suddenly reminding him he was oddly cold.

The woman tugged on his arm. "Come. I will take you in the house."

Tristan opened his eyes once more, the waning light casting her features in an amber glow. Even still, he could see a mixture of trepidation and worry scattered across her face.

"No, thank you."

"No?" Those flashing eyes grew wider.

He rolled to his side, and tried to find the numbing fog once more. Blackness crept in on his vision and he closed his eyes, longing to surrender to it. "Please, may I just die on your porch?"

The woman made a startled noise, and then everything faded into the abyss.

Chapter Three

"Mama!" Opal flung open the rear door and called through the house, casting another look at the sodden soldier pooling water on the porch. Where had he come from? The very river itself?

Mama scurried out of the dining room, black skirts swishing around her ankles. "What's happened?"

As Mama gained the threshold, Opal flung her arm out at the soldier.

"Oh, my!" Mama glanced around. "Where did he come from?"

"I have no idea. He asked if he could die on our porch."

Mama's eyes rounded. "What now?"

"Just as I said." Opal knelt beside the man, a fellow with a red-brown beard and a mop of matching hair. The lines of his face were pleasing, and many would have considered him handsome if not for the haunted eyes that stabbed at her whenever they were open. Like muddy pools of empty despair, they had tugged at her heart. What manner of pain must he be in to have eyes like that?

"What are we going to do with him?"

Opal gently parted the hair on his scalp, squinting in the failing light to see what had caused the seep of blood. "I think he's had a head injury. He didn't seem to quite understand where he was."

Mama rounded the man and nudged her toe at the dog stretched out at his side, but the creature merely groaned and scooted closer to the man. Mama scowled at it. "Wonder why the dog has plastered himself to this fellow?"

Opal rocked back on her heels. "Perhaps it senses the man is in need."

Mama looked dubious. "Well, then, I suppose they can keep one another company."

"We can't leave him on the porch."

"And what do you propose we do with him? He's obviously in no mind or condition to remove himself."

A strange tightness coiled in her chest. It wouldn't be charitable of them to leave him out here in such a condition. Besides, he'd seemed confused, but not dangerous. "We shall take him inside."

Mama tilted her nose in the air. "I'll not have some mad soldier loose in the house." She gestured to him. "Besides, that is no little fellow. How do you propose to move him?"

Opal had no answer to that. He likely weighed as much as she and Mama combined, solid as he looked. And with him in so deep a sleep, he would be like trying to move a dead horse. She nibbled her lip. "Perhaps we can get him into something dry, bring a blanket, and hope he wakes in the night. Then he can come inside."

The startled sound that came from Mama's throat

almost made Opal smile. She knew the words Mama would say before they passed her lips.

"You mean to undress a strange man? What in all of creation has gotten into you?"

"He needs help," she said with a sigh, rising to look Mama in the eyes. "We cannot in good conscious just let him suffer and die when we are able to take care of him. We'll not be like the men who passed by the beaten man on the road, will we? Here before us is a broken man in as much need as the man the Good Samaritan took under his care."

Mama's eyes flickered. Opal pressed on. "Is it not written, whoever sees his brother in need, but has no compassion for him, how does the love of God remain in him?"

Mama sighed. "Very well." She pointed a long finger at Opal. "But you shall not be the one to remove his garments. I'll not have my only daughter scandalized."

Such had been Mama's argument against Opal volunteering to aid at any hospitals during the war. She'd said there would be plenty of older married women who could tend to the soldiers like sons. A pretty young daughter must stay safely at home.

Imprisoned at home, it had often felt like. How she'd been thrilled when Ella had come to Greenville. But knowing Mama was correct, Opal dipped her chin. "Thank you, Mama. That is most generous of you. I shall fetch a blanket."

"Some of your father's clothes, as well." The words came so softly Opal almost missed them.

She hesitated. "Are you certain?"

"It's only a loan, mind you, but it seems this fellow has need of them for tonight." Mama kept her eyes trained on the soldier, and Opal could only wonder at what thoughts plagued her.

She passed through the house, her mind aflutter. The shadows clung to the upper hall, but she had no need of a lantern. Not only did the empty space offer no furniture to trip her, she could have walked these floors with her eyes closed and not falter. She slipped her hand over the cool knob of the door to Daddy's chamber. Mama had allowed no one to open it since they'd learned of his death that fateful day in the fall of '64.

Taking a deep breath, Opal pushed open the door and stepped inside. Little remained, the writing desk, washbasin, and marble-top chifforobe having long since been carried off. Only the massive carved canopy bed, missing its feather mattress, and armoire still graced the space. Opal pried open the armoire doors with a protesting squeak, feeling as though she trespassed. Inside, Daddy's clothes had been neatly stacked and hung.

Opal ran her finger over the material, a lump forming in her throat both for the loss of her father and the reverent care Mama had put into the only remaining thing left of her beloved husband. If Mama had not taken these clothes out to wash and press in anticipation of Daddy's furlough, then they wouldn't have been in a dirty heap in the washroom when the Yanks invaded. But Daddy had never made it home for his furlough. Mama had finished washing and pressing the items when the Yanks had gone, then gently placed them here and locked the room away.

Pushing aside the memories, Opal plucked a linen shirt and a pair of trousers from the collection and closed the doors. The more intimate items the soldier would just have to do without, as she could not bring herself to pilfer them. She closed the door to Daddy's room and stepped across the hall into her own, grabbing the newly finished quilt she'd spent the evenings working on. Fashioned from the usable portions of her old gowns, it was an array of feminine, if not somewhat worn, colors. She'd hoped it would be large enough to cover her bed for the winter, but she'd run out of fabric. Still, it would do.

She plucked it from the hand-hewn chair one of the servants had left behind and scurried back down the stairs. She found Mama standing over the soldier, arms crossed.

"What took you so long?"

"Sorry, Mama." Opal handed over the quilt and garments, then turned her back on the proceedings.

Twice Mama's sounds of strain tempted her to turn, but she knew better than to offer aid. Finally, long after full dark had settled on them, Mama pronounced him finished, her tone mournful.

Opal turned to look at him, dressed in Daddy's black trousers and a linen shirt. She leaned closer. "What have you tied on him?"

Mama stared down at the five black ribbons secured around his upper left arm. "I knew he would not want them removed, so I put them back."

A weight settled on her. Where a widow donned

widow's rags, a man might tie a strip of cloth in remembrance of those lost. *Five. So many to lose.* Her heart wrenched for his heartache, and she watched him for a moment, having nothing to offer but a silent prayer the Almighty might grant healing for his soul as well as his body. Opal knelt beside him, the silver slant of moonlight barely caressing his face. "I shall sit with him."

"Of course you will not!" Mama shook herself from her contemplations. "I'll not have my daughter out alone with a man in the night."

Agitation swirled. "Mama." She waited until she gained Mama's gaze. "This is hardly a situation in which propriety is of utmost importance." She gestured to the man. "He is no danger, and it's no different from nurses sitting at the side of patients. I would like to know if he wakes in the night." Her throat suddenly tightened but she cleared it away. "And if it happens he passes from this world to the next, I do not think he should be alone when he does."

Pain flickered across Mama's face, the depth of it evident even in the scant light. Did she wonder again how Daddy's final moments had passed, as Opal now did? Left out in the battlefield as he had been, had anyone been at his side? Opal pushed the thought away. It would do them no good to dwell on it. They could do nothing for Daddy, but this man could still benefit from their kindness.

"Perhaps you are right." Looking resigned, Mama crossed her arms. "We will stay with him through the night and pray he wakes."

She shifted from one foot to the other, not wishing to argue but concerned all the same. "And what of your condition?"

Mama was silent for a time. "This leaves me in a very difficult situation, you know that don't you?"

"I do, Mama. But if it makes you feel more comfortable, I shall sit just inside the threshold and keep the rifle by my side. Should he appear dangerous in any way, I shall bolt the door."

Mama hesitated a moment longer, then finally relented. "Very well. I will leave my door open. If he as much as stirs, you are to call for me. Is that understood?"

"Yes, ma'am."

Mama turned and disappeared into the house, leaving the rear door open for the bugs to find their way in. Her bout with the fever in '63 made Mama all the more wary of the ever-present mosquitoes, and they had often endured the heat to avoid the insects. Threadbare sheets had replaced the mosquito netting over Mama's bed, but the nuisances still found their way within.

Once Mama started toward her bed, Opal hurried into the library and reached up into the hollow of the fireplace. Spreading her feet wide for balance, she thrust her arm up through the chimney opening until she felt the smooth wood of the rifle hanging against the brick. She tugged it off the hook and maneuvered the length of it out of the hiding place.

It could do with a good cleaning, and she had no idea if it would even fire. But that didn't matter. She had no intention of shooting the poor fellow. Scare him, maybe, if she really had to, but mostly she retrieved it to make Mama feel at ease.

She set the rifle down at the threshold of the rear door and then stepped back onto the porch. A chorus of frogs and nighttime creatures began to swell in discordant harmony, the sounds of the night familiar and yet always a bit eerie. The dog whimpered, thumping his tail against the wood.

"You have taken a liking to this one, I see." Opal shook her head. What was she doing talking to a dog? Had she truly grown that lonely? The dog raised its head from its paws and lifted furry ears at her, as though it was just as surprised as she.

Mama had draped the man in Opal's quilt and tucked it under his chin. His socked feet stuck out of the bottom, battered boots sitting neatly by his side. Sweat slid down the nape of her neck. Likely this fellow would not welcome the added warmth of a quilt in the August night, now that he was dry. She pulled it off him, rolling it into a makeshift pillow.

Kneeling at his side, she slipped her hand underneath his head and gently lifted. He groaned, turning his face toward her.

"Is that you, Millie?"

"Shhh. Don't talk now."

His eyelids fluttered. "Saw…an angel."

She slid the quilt under his head, and he sank into it with a sigh. "Ummm. And she smelled like honey."

The man had grown delirious. Opal leaned closer, trying to squint at the wound on his head. Should she get a lamp and try to tend it now, or wait for Mama and the morning's light?

He thrashed, arms flying out. "No! Don't!"

Startled, Opal stumbled back, falling on her backside. The dog whimpered, and then stuck its snout under the man's arm, nudging him. The fellow mumbled again and turned his head. She got on her knees, watching him.

He flung his arms out again, then grew still. She waited for a time, and when it seemed he had settled, she moved closer once again. His breathing turned even. She waffled for a moment between attempting to rouse him and letting him sleep, and finally decided she should find a lantern and see what she could do with that wound.

Leaving him to the insistent canine company, she stepped over the rifle and back into the house once more. Gathering the items she needed from the parlor, Opal struck a match as she walked, lighting the wick and turning it up enough to create a warm pool of light. Using her hand to shield the flame since the lantern had lost the glass chimney in a fit of her clumsiness, she stepped back out onto the porch and knelt beside their unexpected...uh...*porch* guest.

He never stirred as she parted his hair. A long gash snaked through his scalp from hairline to crown. Deep, it oozed blood and had been caked with hair. She wrinkled her nose. He really could do with a good haircut, and though she didn't know much by way of doctoring, even she could tell the wound needed to be sewn together. Dare she? Knowing she didn't fare all that well with a needle even in cloth, flesh would be an entirely different matter.

But Mama certainly wouldn't have the stomach for it. She grabbed the lamp and made for the parlor again. Better she just do it now without Mama's scrutinizing gaze. If she were lucky, he might even remain unconscious through the entire thing.

Pulling open the drawer in the hutch, Opal fished out her sewing kit and a pair of scissors and secured them in her skirt pocket. Then she made her way to the kitchen and looped a pail of water and a rag over her arm. Supplies ready, she stepped lightly through the deep shadows of night, her pulse quickening.

She found the man exactly as she'd left him, dog at his side and breathing evenly. He looked peaceful in sleep. A wide forehead graced by neat but manly eyebrows shielded a straight nose and sturdy cheekbones. The dog thumped its tail and gave a whimpering noise as though to say it had taken note of her overlong assessment.

With a huff, she shook her foot at the dog. "Shoo." The mongrel merely yipped at her and thumped its tail. "Oh, good heavens," Opal mumbled. It seemed the furry creature could be just as stubborn.

Ignoring it, she situated her tools, taking hold of the scissors first. Hopefully the fellow hadn't formed an attachment to his damp locks. With quick movements, she gathered up sections of his hair and snipped it off close to his scalp. Even when she lifted his head and turned it from side to side, his deep breathing didn't change.

Satisfied he would not wake while she tended him,

Opal carefully set to shearing his locks and freeing bits of hair from the gash. When his hair was neatly clipped, the beard looked rather out of hand, so she trimmed it back as well.

There. A fine job. Hopefully he would think the same. She dipped the rag in the tepid well water and wrung it out. Keeping the lantern close, she gently washed the bits of dirt and hair from his gash until nothing but pink flesh remained. Now for the hard part.

It took three tries to thread the needle with shaking hands, but she finally got it. She snipped the end of a length of thread free from the spool and tied the ends. Closing her eyes, Opal drew a long, calming breath.

Please steady my hands. She peeked at the man. *And, please, Lord, let him not wake.*

Before she could talk herself out of it, Opal slipped the needle into the tender skin at the man's hairline. He moaned a little, but didn't move. Lips moving in silent prayer as she worked, she made tight stitches all the way down the length of the wound, binding the edges of flesh like the pieces of her quilt. If only she'd had a little whiskey to pour on it. But hope and prayer would have to do.

The dog watched her with careful eyes as she cleaned her hands and set the bucket aside. Then she gathered the sewing tools back into her pocket, retrieved the lantern, and settled down in the doorway to keep watch.

Chapter Four

Tristan gained awareness in spurts. First it started with the realization that he lay prone on something hard. Then he floated back to the surface of consciousness to note the warmth of sunshine across his face and the chirp of birds. Their song filled his ears, a reminder that he had survived whatever darkness had taken hold of him. He sifted through his memory, looking for something more than a sense that he had somehow escaped death, but found nothing solid.

Someone hummed softly, further tugging him back to the world he wasn't sure he wished to set weary eyes on once more. He waited as his senses slowly returned to him, listening. The humming shifted into a mournful song, its lyrics about God's grace wrapped in a soulful melody. Thoughts clamored for attention, but for the moment he could only drift in the current of that voice.

As he became more aware, a sensation in his scalp distracted him from the song. It both itched and burned, and his fingers twitched to scratch it. The singing stopped. Tristan stilled. Best he find out more about his surroundings before revealing his awareness.

"Ah, good. You are awake."

Relief flooded the feminine voice in such a way he forgot to be annoyed and cracked his eyes open against the blistering sun. It took several blinks to focus on the face that hovered over him. He squinted, the woman seeming vaguely familiar.

"We didn't know if you would make it through the night, bad off as you were." She leaned closer, peering at his head. "Think you can stand and come inside?"

He stared at her for a moment, then slowly turned his head from side to side. He wouldn't go about sullying this lady's home.

"Very well. We can wait a bit longer until you gain your strength."

He grunted. Couldn't this woman see he was fine? He pulled himself into a sitting position, then immediately regretted it. Pain stabbed through his skull, and his stomach roiled.

"Easy, there, sir. We can wait." She placed a hand on his back to steady him. "I'll fetch you some water, if you think you can stay awake."

Tristan placed his hands behind him to support his weight, feeling himself steady. The woman waited a moment and then scurried off in a rustle of feminine fabric. He wiggled his toes. Had he lost his boots in the river? They weren't much to be had, but they were better than socks.

He frowned. These were not his uniform grays. Alarm sprang up and he gripped his left arm. Fingers brushing over the ribbons, he counted them. Still five.

A few moments later, the lady returned. "Mama changed you into some of my father's dry things, but she was careful to retie your bands."

Tristan lowered his hand from where he still caressed them. He folded his legs, eyeing the woman as she handed him a cup. She studied him as openly as he studied her. She had thick hair piled on top of her head, hinting that it would likely fall past her hips if it were unbound. Gentle features soft with femininity housed warm cinnamon eyes that seemed to stare right through him.

He looked away and sipped the clear water. He would never again take for granted the clean goodness of well water after all the times he'd guzzled straight from a stream.

"I'm Miss Opal Martin, and this is my home, Riverbend."

Past the grass stirring in the gentle breeze, the mighty Mississippi bent an arm around the property, crooking it in an elbow like a mother with her child. "Adequately named," he said, his voice raspy. He cleared his throat.

"My father thought so." There was a smile in her voice, but sorrow as well. Most likely she counted him among her lost, though she didn't wear mourning blacks. "Even though many people told him he built it too close to the river."

Tristan set the cup aside, glad for the soothing refreshment. "Likely did." He reached up to scratch at the cut on his head, only to find his hair no longer laid in clumps along his forehead. Probing, he found the source of the itching. He looked back at the woman. What had she said her name was?

She knelt beside him, yellow skirts pooling around her knees. "I needed to trim it so I could stitch the wound." Her voice held both apology and challenge, and he nearly chuckled.

The sensation surprised him, and he forced it down with a scowl. "You changed my clothes, cut my hair, and stitched my scalp while I slept?"

"And trimmed your beard."

His fingers immediately went to test her words. Even without a mirror, he could tell she'd done a fine job. He should say so, give her some form of gratitude, but all he could do was stare at her.

"But it was Mama who changed your clothing," she said, though she'd given him that information already. Did she fear he would think her loose, undressing a man without his consent? He reached for the bands on his arms, rubbing the frayed end of the last one between his fingers. What would he think if Millie had done something like that?

"We were afraid you would die."

Her voice pulled him from his contemplations, and he leveled his gaze on her once more. "Would have been just fine for you to let me, Miss…." What was it? Marion?

"Martin. Opal Martin." She leaned in closer, and he caught another whiff of what reminded him of honey and fresh bread. "Do you remember how you came to be in the river, sir?"

She probed at him with questions as though he had not just said she should have let him die in peace. He had the distinct feeling this particular little sparrow would not leave him be until she had satisfied herself with his well-being. He smirked. If that was the case, she might never be rid of him. The smile disappeared as suddenly as it began.

Miss Martin scrunched her forehead. "Can you tell me your name?"

Of course he could. Did the woman think him daft? "Lieutenant..." he trailed off and shook his head, sending another wave of pain skittering over his skull. War was over. He'd mustered out. The rank he'd earned on the field meant nothing once the band of volunteers had been broken and turned away to pick up the shattered pieces of their lives. "*Mister* Tristan Stuart."

"And where are you from, Mr. Stuart?"

The words tasted bitter as he spat them out. "Used to be from Rolling Fork."

She seemed to contemplate the words, turning them over behind those pretty eyes. "My father knew some people from there. Forty miles is not all that far, but we didn't see them much. Do you know the Parish family?"

Bile rolled in his stomach. "Did."

Pain flared in her eyes and she nodded. "Of course. My apologies. Many were brave in their attempts to stop Porter's invasion of the Yazoo." She shook her head. "Who would have ever thought those gunships would have been able to squeeze down Deer Creek?" Her voice took on a faraway quality, as though she remembered the day that had changed his life.

Brave, certainly. But failed attempts, all. He clenched his jaw. "Lot of good it did. Got those old ironsides stuck solid, but with Sherman driving his forces in, there was nothing they could really do. Nothing could stop that devil on his drive to the sea."

"They made Grant abandon his plans and retreat," she said softly, as though that made any difference. Vicksburg had been lost a short time later regardless of their efforts.

Rage flicked through him, a familiar burning as hot as Sherman's flames. He tried to squelch it, but the widening of her eyes told him he'd failed. She gave a little shiver and watched his eyes for a moment, then drew a breath and leaned back away from him.

"Well, it would seem you have use of your memory and senses."

He lifted his eyebrows, feeling the stitches at his hairline contract.

She offered a small smile. Not the kind that spoiled belles flaunted, but the tempered kind of a woman familiar with the woes of the world. "With your injury," she said, gesturing to his head, "I wanted to be sure."

Tristan looked around at the quiet lawn, trying to remember exactly what had occurred between stepping in the river and waking up here. But he wouldn't tell the lady that, lest she begin fussing over him again. He rolled his legs under him and sat on his knees. She moved forward as though to help him, but then seemed to think better of it, allowing him the dignity of rising to his own feet.

Once there, he felt a bit unstable, and his first step had him wobbling.

"Mama!" Miss Martin gave a shout and then

slipped her small frame underneath his arm, snaking her own arm across his lower back and using herself as a crutch to steady him.

Tristan grabbed his head, the pounding increasing.

"Shoo, you!" Miss Martin hissed, shaking her skirts at something.

Still holding the palm of his hand into his left eye, Tristan followed the movement to a scraggly dog with mud-colored fur staring up at him. It slashed its tail through the air, ears perked up.

Tristan laughed at the absurdity of the situation, the response a near forgotten memory. Miss Martin stilled, and he could feel her eyes upon him even as he kept his gaze on the dog. The bit of mirth dissipated, like a burst of light swallowed by darkness.

"This fellow here found me on the river bank," Tristan mused. "Think he was the one that led me here."

Miss Martin scowled at the creature. "He's been hanging around here for weeks now, and we can't seem to be rid of him."

"Oh! He has come to!" Another lady's voice, this one sounding older, came from behind him, and in a moment, Tristan found himself ensconced in a feminine embrace from both sides.

He stared down at the dog, wondering if the canine could sense his humiliation at having to be held up by two small women. The dog tilted its head to the side, as though mocking his predicament.

The women turned, angling him toward the door leading into the house. The dog bounded on their heels, and Miss Martin admonished it again. The dog plopped down on the porch, chin on its paws. If he didn't know better, Tristan would swear the poor thing pouted at the injustice of not being allowed inside.

A fitting sentiment. Just like the dog, Tristan was unfit to sully this place. He attempted to still his feet. "I will not intrude upon your home, ladies."

The women paused for only an instant, then without a word began tugging on him once more. He forced words through his teeth, the ache in his head making his will weak. "Just deposit me in the yard."

The older woman, clad in blacks and obviously Miss Martin's mother, barked a laugh. "Don't be ridiculous. What kind of people do you think we are, leaving an injured man out in the yard?"

Miss Martin leaned forward to peer at her mother across Tristan's borrowed shirt, but she said nothing. Even as he protested, he allowed the women to take him across the threshold. "I could remain on the porch, then. It is enough."

"Nonsense, boy. Quit your bellyaching. You'll take your ease in the parlor until you can get your feet steady beneath you."

It took more concentration than he cared to admit to keep a hold of his consciousness. He could not allow himself to fall limp upon these women and leave them with a heap of wasted soldier upon their floor.

By the time they finally eased him down onto a couch, his head pounded furiously and his stomach revolted. He leaned back without resistance as they stretched him onto his back, fussing with staccato whispers at one another. He meant to thank them, but his lips seemed too thick to move, his voice lost.

Then the swelling warmth of darkness beckoned him once more, and he slipped into the peace of nothingness.

"That boy doesn't look well," Mama stated, as though Opal couldn't see that for herself.

Healthy men didn't sprawl across the settee with one arm hanging off and knuckles brushing the rug. Opal studied him for a moment longer. "He seems plenty lucid, though I still worry with that wound on his head. There's no telling how bad it really is."

Mama eyed him as though he might spring up from his position at any moment. "Yes, you never can tell what a blow to the head will do to a person."

"Do you remember when little Peter Wilson fell out of that tree?" Opal wagged her head. "He wasn't right after that for a long time."

"He was never the same." Mama eyed Mr. Stuart again. "I hope he hasn't gone mad."

Mad with grief, perhaps. She had seen it etched across his features and shining in his eyes. "I think not. He answered my questions well enough, and seemed normal."

Mama lifted her eyebrows in that way she had that told Opal Mama was sorely displeased. "I see you decided to do more than sit at the threshold with the rifle."

The rifle. She'd forgotten all about it. Her eyes betrayed her, darting toward the parlor door.

Mama waved a hand, her critical gaze dissolving as quickly as a rare Mississippi snow. "I already put it back. Wouldn't be worth much more than a stick to whack him with, anyway."

Opal suppressed a smile. "His head had a nasty gash. I thought it might be best to stitch him up whilst he couldn't do much about it."

Mama opened her mouth to reply, no doubt with a quick retort about Opal's foolishness, but a rap at the door stalled her words. Mama thrust her chin toward the foyer.

Running a hand down her hopelessly rumpled dress, Opal moved to the door, annoyed the mongrel that insisted upon living with them had once again failed to do the one thing that made it useful—announce intruders.

She pulled open the door, displeased yet unsurprised to see the oiled Mr. Weir upon the porch. Though Mama had given him permission to return, it was barely a decent morning hour. So much for the hope he would change his mind about Riverbend and move on.

His eyes roamed over her, lingering on her hair. Opal resisted the urge to reach up to smooth it. Instead, she lifted her nose in an imitation of the look Mama always made when she wanted someone to wither. "Yes?"

"I've come as your mother requested." He gave a small bow, as though he was an honored guest and not an unscrupulous vulture.

"This is not a good time." She waved him back, making certain her meaning could not be missed. "You'll simply have to return later." *Or not at all.* "Mama is currently indisposed."

He darted a gaze behind her, and even before Mama spoke Opal could sense her presence. She withheld a sigh.

"Good morning, sir. We haven't yet had our breakfast, and I am not prepared to entertain at this hour," Mama said calmly, sweeping past Opal and outside. Mr. Weir stepped back to allow her room. "But I will speak with you a moment on the porch, if that suits you."

"Certainly. I won't take up much of your time."

Mama cast Opal a look over her shoulder. "Why don't you freshen up and see to the breakfast? This shan't take long."

Opal seamed her lips to keep unwise words properly withheld and returned inside. She pressed her ear to the door, but Mama had likely suspected as much. All she heard was, "Come, Mr. Weir, you may escort me on a walk while we discuss your intentions."

Opal gritted her teeth. May as well see to her morning necessities and return to Mr. Stuart, lest he thrash about again and deposit himself on the floor. Perhaps she might even get him to eat something. Upstairs, she snagged a threadbare green gown and tugged it over her head. Then she freed the pins from her hair, shook out her locks, and twisted the length of it into a long braid before wrapping the plait around her head and securing it once more. She'd need to take the yellow gown to wash, knowing it would take days to fully dry in this humidity.

Once, such things never concerned her. She'd had a wardrobe full of dresses and servants to launder them. Now she had no servants and only two gowns to trade out. And this yellow one would soon need more mending. She'd lost enough weight that she could probably bring in the seams to keep them from fraying open.

Downstairs, she peeked out the window. Mama had paused in the drive, listening intently to whatever the carpetbagger said. Opal couldn't see his face, but he gestured with his hands.

A noise drew her back to the immediate problem at hand. Mr. Stuart groaned, and she pulled herself from the glass panes flanking the front door. Praying Mama wouldn't do anything rash or foolish, Opal stepped back into the parlor.

Tristan sat on the dainty couch holding his head, silently cursing both the pain and his slips in and out of awareness. A swish of fabric announced one of his guardians, and he was unable to contain his frustration with himself as he looked up. The glance must have been enough to melt iron, but Miss Martin merely bristled.

"Are you well?"

He made a noise low in his throat. "Do I look well?"

"You do not. Best you lie down again."

He pressed his palm against the throbbing in his left eye and glared at her with the other. She had no cause to stare at him with both concern and irritation. He had asked her to leave him outside. It wasn't his fault he tarnished her parlor. "Why?"

Miss Martin placed her hands upon her hips. "*Why?* Because you have a head injury and are having trouble keeping consciousness."

Something sparked in his mind, reminding him of how a gentleman should treat a lady, and of the man he had been before the war chiseled at all of his smooth edges. She didn't deserve such treatment. She only meant to help. Tristan closed his eyes, trying to find the old him he'd nearly forgotten. He lowered his hand, and when he opened his eyes again, he hoped she would see something better.

Instead, she looked even more concerned and moved closer, leaning near him as she narrowed her gaze. He pulled back. "What are you doing, Miss Martin?"

"I am looking to see if your eyes are too large."

"Beg your pardon?" Her smell tickled his nose, and he tried to lean farther away, lest he taint her, but he could find no more room in which to do so. Still she came closer.

Her lips pursed. "Your pupils appear normal, just...." She let the sentence die, leaving him to stare at her, unable to tear his gaze away.

"Just what?" She was close enough that if he'd had the notion, he could have kissed her. The thought caught him by surprise, and he closed his eyes to try to erase the sight of her.

She sighed, her breath wafting across his face and smelling like sassafras. "Just…haunted."

He barked a bitter laugh, watching her as she stepped back. "That so? I reckon they are no different from any other man who has seen his friends dismembered, seen brothers in arms bleed out in agony, and listened to the screams of families as they burned in their homes."

Her features paled, and he cursed his foolishness. Had four years of horror erased *all* that he had once known of being a gentleman? His mother would be ashamed. Tristan searched for the words that could convey even a portion of his regret at having soiled her, but the front door opened and she spun away.

In a flash of green skirts she disappeared, leaving him alone with his wretchedness. Whispers floated in from the entryway, too low for him to decipher.

"What!" Miss Martin's screech bounced off the walls and slammed into him.

Tristan clenched his jaw and tried to gain his feet, but no sooner had he found them than a wave of dizziness had him dropping back to the couch.

"You have lost your mind!"

Tristan held his throbbing head. The thud of shoes through the house beat in near rhythm with his pulse, followed by the squeak and slam of the rear door.

Then he was left alone in the silence once more.

Chapter Five

O pal ground her teeth so hard they hurt. She spun around in the kitchen, arms folding across her heaving chest. "What has gotten into you, Mama?"

Mama looked at her calmly, hands clasped together. "This is a bit of an overreaction, don't you think?"

"No, I don't think it is at all." She rubbed the bridge of her nose. "You're not making any sense."

With a sigh, Mama settled on the top of a flour barrel. "We can't go on like this. I've been thinking for some weeks now that we need to figure out a way to improve our condition. It seems that answer has arrived on our porch."

Opal paced the kitchen, her nerves too aflame to stay in one place. "I know things are hard, but we've been better off than most."

Mama watched her pace. "Indeed. We still have a standing home and land to sell to free us from this desolate place. It is a blessing we should use."

"But....Daddy built this house for you. How can...?" She let the words drift away on the thick morning air. The pain in Mama's eyes was enough.

"I must learn to look ahead, not behind. And I

must think of you, and the quality of your future."

"But I'm—"

Mama held up a hand to stay her words. "You are a brave girl, and I know you put on a smile for me. But a young woman should be attending balls and entertaining suitors. She should be preparing for her own life, not taking care of a widowed mother in a stripped plantation." Tears glistened in Mama's eyes. "I have nothing more I can give you."

Opal stilled in her pacing and knelt in front of Mama's gown. She reached out and took one of her hands. "This is our home. And as you said, many were left without even that. Where would we go?"

"North. To my cousin Eunice."

The words took a moment to sink in, as though they were grains too large for the sifter. "Who?"

"I have a distant cousin in Massachusetts. She also lost her husband in the war."

She stared at Mama. Then hardly believing she had to say the words to a stout secessionist, Opal said, "A Yankee?"

"And a relative."

Opal rose and moved away from Mama, choosing instead to lean against the table. "You cannot be serious."

"I have been sending letters to her for the past several weeks discussing the possibility."

"What letters?"

Mama raised her eyebrows. "You don't know everything I do. I sent a letter to Eunice with my condolences after I learned from Aunt Mable that she'd lost her husband at Gettysburg. We exchanged letters after that, and she mentioned us coming to live with her."

"We can't just move up north to live with a stranger!"

"She's family." Mama lowered her eyes. "And she is a widow living alone who could do with the company."

Her heart clenched. Did she not provide Mama the company she needed?

"And," Mama continued, "Massachusetts is nearly untouched by the ravishing of war. We could start a new life there away from the destruction."

The thought was more tempting than Opal cared to admit. Could they really start over? Live in a place where lawless bandits were not lurking in the shadows on every trip to a burned town? Could they once again wear fine clothes and go to tea with friends?

"With the money from Mr. Weir," Mama said, her tone meant to be soothing, "we could purchase traveling tickets, and when we get there, new wardrobes for us both. You could attend social functions again."

"With Yankees."

Mama sniffed. "You say that as though you are not already friendly with Yanks."

Opal's eyes widened.

"Or have you forgotten Major Remington served in Yankee Blues?"

"That's different." Opal made a face, even though Mama's words rang true. "What do you think will happen if we move north into enemy territory? Do you not think we would, at the very least, be ridiculed and shunned?"

Sadness flitted across Mama's eyes. "There is no more *enemy territory*. We are one nation again. Better we suffer the consequences of the war with snide words than with a sparse home and not enough supplies for winter."

Mama rose and brushed off her skirts. "Trust me in this. It will be for the best." She turned away, but not before Opal saw the tears glistening in her eyes.

Opal sat in silence for several moments before slathering slices of thick bread with jam and taking the platter to the parlor. She found Mr. Stuart asleep once again, so she left the platter on the low table next to him and went to her room to gather her things.

She stepped out into the warm day and tied the strings of her bonnet. Spine straight, she made it all the way down the porch steps before sighing and turning back to the house. As much as she'd like to storm off without a word, she wouldn't frighten Mama. If they'd had any paper, she would have penned a note, but that was just another of the things they'd learned to live without.

She opened the front door to see Mama coming down the stairs.

"I thought I heard the door. Has Mr. Weir returned already? He said he wished some time to consider his options, but perhaps he didn't need it."

Opal fought back her annoyance with the hope in Mama's tone. "No. I came back to tell you I am going to visit with Ella for a little while."

Mama scrunched her brow as though she were about to protest, but then gave a small nod. "Very well. I will look after the soldier."

"I left him some bread. Hopefully once he eats, he will regain a measure of his strength."

"Let us hope." She flicked a glance at the parlor, worry evident in the tight pull of her lips. "Be careful, and keep a sharp eye."

"Don't worry, Mama. It is not far. I will be careful."

Mama nodded and Opal hurried back out of the door. The walk was peaceful, if not stifling, and gave her time to think even as she kept a wary eye out for danger. Part of her could see the appeal in starting over in lands unstained by this war. But at the same time, she could not fathom leaving her home behind, even amid the struggles. Besides, Massachusetts would be far too cold.

Sweat collected in her hairline and trailed a line down her cheek as though in defiance of her thoughts. Perhaps summers without the constant mosquitoes and oppressive heat wouldn't be so bad after all. She could stay inside all winter. She swished her skirts as she walked, stirring up little clouds of dust with her hem.

As she neared the Remington lands, the soulful sounds of the farmers carried across the fields. Once booming only with cotton, they now also grew corn and other food crops to help ease the shortage. Dark-skinned men and women toiled under the hot sun, earning their wages.

Mr. Remington had worked out some kind of arrangement with the government that had allowed him enough seed to start anew, and Ella had worked out deals with scores of freed slaves that paid them both in coin from the crop sales as well as a portion of the harvest itself.

Some of them eyed her as she passed, but none stilled from their labors. Their song followed her down the river road for a time, becoming but a wordless melody by the time she reached the grand gates of Belmont.

The large brick home beckoned her to the comfort of her dear friend's counsel, and she hurried her steps. Edged in magnolia trees, the yard teemed with flowers that perfumed the air with their fragrance. The house windows stood open, and Ella's melodious voice drifted past the sills.

Opal rapped on the door and waited for Sibby to greet her. The nursemaid was quick in her duty, and in only a couple of moments, her features appeared.

"Well, if it ain't Miss Opal done come to call." The smile on her wide lips faltered and she glanced behind Opal. "Your momma done come wit you this time?"

"No, Mama is seeing to our…company."

"Company?"

"Sibby!" Ella's voice came from behind little Lee's nursemaid. "Aren't you going to let the poor girl inside?"

Sibby made a face Ella couldn't see and pulled the door wide, gesturing Opal inside. "We was just talkin' is all."

Ella tucked a strand of her fire and gold hair back into the mass of curls pinned to her head. "Well, that can be done in the parlor. You're letting the bugs in."

Sibby rolled her eyes and then reached for the baby on Ella's hip. "Best you give little man to me, then, since you got talkin' to do. Miss Opal here has company, and from the look she done had on her face, it's interestin' company." She hummed as she took the boy up the stairs.

Opal waved to him, and he smiled with chubby cheeks back over Sibby's shoulder.

"Company?" Ella asked, moving toward the parlor.

It never ceased to amaze her how the Remington home remained so intact. In here, one could almost forget the war. But then, the Remingtons had encountered their own problems. Who was she to say the reasoning behind the Lord's doings?

"You missed quite a lot of excitement after you left," Opal said, sitting on the settee in the ladies' parlor.

"Aye?" Ella arranged her skirts and tilted her head. "Well, isn't that just the way it goes?" She laughed, the Scottish lilt to her voice enchanting.

Opal sighed, slouching back against the settee, glad Mama wasn't here to scold her. "I don't even know where to begin."

"How about with what happened after I got in my carriage?"

Opal laughed, Ella's mischievous tone teasing her from her worry. "First it was the carpetbagger, then it was the dying soldier."

Ella leaned forward, her eyes wide. "Do tell!"

"No sooner had the dust settled from your carriage than this dandy in a fine suit appeared on the porch. He claimed that his horse had thrown a shoe, and he had come to ask for help."

"I didn't see a horse on the road." Ella scrunched her nose. "But then, I wasn't really looking for one, either."

Opal let her eyes drift over the papered walls and the intricately carved molding lining the high ceiling. "He just wanted to look at the house. I caught him sniffing around like a hound." She waved a hand. "In fact, it was the dog that let me know the man prowled around the side of the house."

Ella put a hand to her throat. "What nerve!"

"It gets worse. Mama came outside and started talking to him. He wants to buy the house."

She expected a gasp, or a scowl, or…*something*, but instead Ella's forehead only crinkled in thought. "He wishes to buy Riverbend? At what price?"

"I don't know. What does it matter?"

Ella rubbed a stray curl between her fingers. "Oh, just wondering what a dandy might offer. I've heard tell that they are trying to take advantage of desperate families and purchase property for well below what it's worth." She pursed her lips. "Or, rather, what it *used* to be worth."

"Whatever he offered, it appealed to Mama. She's considering it."

Now the gasp of surprise came. "But where would you go?"

Opal groaned, knowing she sounded too much like a petulant child rather than a lady, but still not caring. Ella was the one person with whom she could relax.

"Massachusetts! Can you believe it? She says she has a distant cousin there who offered for us to come and live with her."

Ella was quiet for several moments. "We will have to pray over it and see. But I do not think Westley would protest if you wished to live here instead."

The notion was tempting, but only for a moment. "I could not leave Mama on her own, nor could I impose on our friendship." She reached across to grasp Ella's hand. "But your generous offer means more to me than you can imagine."

Moisture gathered in Ella's eyes but she blinked it away. "We shall discuss it again after we've had time to think and pray on it. Now, what of this soldier?"

Opal shifted in her seat. "Mr. Tristan Stuart. He must have fallen into the river. Somehow he ended up on my porch with a terrible gash on his head."

"Oh, my!" Ella leaned forward. "Did he survive?"

"He did. I sutured the wound and now he is sleeping in our parlor. Says he's from Rolling Fork."

"Why, Opal." Ella cast her a sidelong glance, her tone turning buttery. "I didn't take you for a nurse."

She returned the bemused smile. "I'm not even good at sewing fabric." She grimaced. "But it had to be done."

A sly look crossed her friend's pale features. "Tell me about this man."

"He has chestnut hair with bits of auburn, and a beard to match."

"Handsome?"

Opal lifted her brows. "I suppose."

"You *suppose?*"

She huffed. "Oh, all right. Yes, he is a nice looking fellow. But he seems…." She let the words trail off, not knowing how to describe the turmoil behind those eyes.

"What?"

"I don't know how to describe it. When he first came, he seemed to think he was someplace else. He asked me if he could die on the porch." A little shiver ran across her arms. "His eyes were so haunted, so filled with agony that I thought my heart would burst just from the sight of them."

"War," Ella said softly. "It does things to a man."

"And it must have cost him a great deal. He wears five black bands upon his arm."

"Aye, that's a lot of loved ones to lose. No doubt it has taken its toll."

"So what am I to do, Ella?"

She studied Opal for a moment, a light dancing in her eyes. "About the soldier or the dandy?"

Opal gained her feet, her nerves fluttering. "Both!"

Ella watched her make tracks around the ladies' parlor, her feet silent on the thick rug. Opal made the fourth round before Ella spoke again. "I don't suppose there is anything you can do about the dandy. Your mother will have to decide what she wants to do with the house. After that, then you will have to measure your options."

Coming to a stop near one of the windows facing the road, Opal moved the curtain aside to look out over the yard. "And the soldier?" she asked, avoiding eye contact.

"Well, now, that is another matter entirely. You have already taken him in, so his well-being is your responsibility."

Opal turned, her skirt flaring. "What do you mean?"

"Are you going to turn him out?"

"Well, no, but…."

"Then you have taken responsibility for him. Perhaps the Lord brought him to your porch instead of any other for a reason. Maybe it is so you can make sure he is properly healed before he returns home." She lifted her shoulders. "Or perhaps there is another reason."

Opal put a hand on her hip. "Such as?"

Ella's lips stretched wide. "You mean a romantic such as yourself hasn't already seen the possibilities?"

Heat raced up her cheeks. "Nonsense."

"Oh, but don't you think it would make a *wonderful story*?"

Her own words, spoken over Ella and Mr. Remington's situation seemed ill-fitting when applied to her own. "I don't even know the man."

Ella laughed. "Like I knew Westley?"

"Ah, well, that was different."

Ella rose and came to wrap her arms around Opal. "I was only teasing you. Come, do not get yourself into a dither."

"I'm not," Opal grumbled, even as she knew it was a lie. Why should she be sensitive to such a ribbing? Perhaps because the loneliness had begun to steal her hopes. Had it not been for war, would she have been married by now? Had a boy of her own settled on her hip?

As though sensing her melancholy thoughts, Ella pulled her closer. "We will pray on it, yes?"

"Yes," Opal agreed, returning the squeeze before stepping away. "We shall pray he is healed, both in body and spirit, and that he will be able to continue on his way hearty."

Ella's lips curled. "Yes, we shall pray for that as well."

They continued to talk about other matters, about how things were going with Westley and Ella, and how Lee had been faring since recovering from his sickness. Each time the conversation drifted toward Mr. Stuart, Opal made sure to steer it away again. She had come seeking her friend's thoughts on the matter, but had been unnerved to realize her own feelings were in a tangled mess. Why should she be in a tizzy about a stranger? No, more likely it was that carpetbagger who had sent her emotions into a swirl.

The sound of scurrying feet brought young Basil to the door with a basket draped over her arm. Her gaze darted to Opal, and the girl's features split into a wide smile. "Morning, Miss Martin." She turned to Ella. "Got them things Miss Sibby said I should get for you."

"What things?"

Basil looked at Opal again, shifting her weight from one foot to the other. "Well, when I done told her 'bout that soldier, she said he'd be needin' some medicine and whatnot...."

Ella tilted her head, and the longer she studied the child, the more the girl shifted. "And tell me, Basil, how is it that Sibby knows about the soldier in the first place?"

The girl's forehead puckered. "Well, now, I was dustin' in the hall like I was supposed to be doin'. Ain't my fault y'all talks so loud."

Ella sighed. "How many times have I told you not to listen in on people's conversations? It isn't ladylike."

"Yes 'um, I know. Sorry."

"Oh, never you mind that, Basil," Opal said. "It is not as though I was sharing any secrets." Though she would remember to do so in her own home if she had any to confide in the future.

Basil grinned and hefted up the basket. "Miss Sibby say these here things would help plenty."

"Thank you," Ella said, giving her red curls a shake. "You may leave them on the table by the door."

Basil bobbed her head and then twirled out the door.

"She means well," Ella said, watching the girl skip away.

"Of course." Opal twisted her hands in her lap. "But I am afraid Mama won't...."

"Your mother still worries you have taken too many things from us?"

"Yes."

Ella leaned forward and took Opal's hand. "And if we should see our neighbor in need, and have the means to help and yet do not, where is the love of God in us?"

Opal giggled. "I used that very verse on Mama yesterday in regard to Mr. Stuart."

"Well then," Ella said, "surely she can see that such

love flows in multiple directions."

"Indeed. But I fear she believes we have become a burden, and our ability to return the favor grows more unreachable each day."

Ella scoffed. "I do not expect you to return anything. You and your mother bore witness at my wedding. Provided a horse for Westley to seek a doctor." She wagged her head. "What are a few provisions compared to that?"

Opal pressed her lips together.

"Has your mother considered Westley's offer?"

"She has, but she has hesitated to turn the fields once again. But now I think I understand why."

"Because she wishes to move to Massachusetts?"

Opal nodded, a lump forming in her throat. "And how can I blame her? She dreads trying to run the plantation without my father, and life with her cousin offers ease, companionship, and an escape from the devastation. How can I be so selfish? How can I in good conscience keep her from such an opportunity?" She hung her head. "But then, how can I go? This is my home, even if it is crumbling. It is terrible of me, but I fear living somewhere unfamiliar."

Ella clasped her hand once more. "Aye, it is a hard thing. What if she was to go and you were to stay?"

"To go she needs to sell the house, and I cannot impose upon you in that way." She held up her hand to stay Ella's protest. "I do not wish to be homeless, Ella, having to depend on the kind hearts of friends. And even if Mama were to somehow go and leave Riverbend to me, I cannot hope to live there on my own."

Ella rose and drew Opal into an embrace. "What does your heart wish for?"

"That my father was still alive."

Pushing her back to arm's length, Ella offered a melancholy smile. "But that is not within your realm of control. Come now, what is it that you long for?"

Opal tried not to choke on the bitter words. "Wish? What good is a wish?" She stepped away from her friend's touch. "I *wish* the war had not come. I *wish* my father had not died. I *wish* my mother wasn't brokenhearted. I *wish* Riverbend hadn't been plundered. I…" She clenched her hands. "I wish *I* had been able to find a fairy tale."

Rather than taking offense, as would have been her right at the venom Opal could not believe she'd allowed to escape the deepest recesses of her heart, Ella merely smiled. "Ah, so now you will admit it."

Opal grimaced. "What?"

"I have long known you to dream of a romance like the kind in those novels your mother hates for you to read."

Heat stirred in her stomach, though there was no warrant for such anger. "She's right. It is utter nonsense."

"Is it? Why, I think you have the makings of a romance worthy of a tale right there on your doorstep."

"Mr. Stuart is not interested in me, and I am not interested in him."

"That so?"

Opal groaned. "Oh, it is so pathetic, Ella! I am lonely, and I wish that I could have what you have. So here I am projecting feelings onto a man *I don't even know* just because he is handsome and at my house!" She lowered her head again, the weight of her own pitiable state seeming heavy across her shoulders. "I have been blessed. We are alive, the house stands, we have food to eat, and friends who shower us in love. I should not feel this way, and I should not think to fling myself at any man within sight."

Ella snorted a laugh. "I have never seen you do anything of the sort, and there are men in town."

She resisted the urge to roll her eyes again. "There are not many men, and most of them are either old or married."

"More have been arriving as they muster out. Just last week two men fawned over you at the general store. You didn't even notice."

"Nonsense."

"It's not. I saw it myself. You didn't catch their gaze even though both were clearly staring." Ella tapped her finger on her chin. "There is more going on here."

Opal snagged her bonnet. "I really must be going."

Ella followed her to the foyer. "Now, don't be sore with me, Opal. I am merely trying to help you sort through things."

"What is there to sort?" Opal peeked into the basket Basil had left. "I don't know the man. Yes, he has these eyes that seem to hold an ocean's depth of…something. But what does that matter?"

Ella grabbed the basket and looped it over Opal's arm. "Did you look into his eyes and feel something in your heart shift in a way that it never has before?"

How could she know that? "I…um…." Opal looked away.

Ella gave her a quick hug and opened the door. "Get on back and take care of him. And while you are walking, be sure to pray over that shifting."

Opal nodded numbly and then made her way out of the house.

Chapter Six

Three weeks later

Tristan sat on the front porch of a house that looked like home but wasn't, scratching the ears of a dog that didn't belong to him, and contemplating how he might help with a problem that shouldn't be affecting him. Yet after weeks under the careful and persistent care of Miss Opal Martin, Tristan found himself not only obligated to help her, but truly wanting to. Something about the way she had weathered his moods yet still looked at him with compassion, and not pity, had begun to pluck out some of his barbs.

He let his fingers untangle a mat of hair on Shadow's ear, and the dog groaned, leaning into him. The day he'd stepped into the river, he'd thought he would never care about anything again. Now he worried about what would happen to a young woman with too big of a heart for her own good. And though it shouldn't be any of his concern, Miss Martin's anxiety over selling her home had Tristan itching to somehow soothe her troubles. Yes, life had a funny way of taking what a man thought he knew and turning it upside down.

The lady's voice drifted from the house, singing a melody that reminded him of long-forgotten mornings in church with his parents, brothers, and Millie. The thought of her wrenched a dark place in him and he clenched his teeth against the pain. Her memory often crept up on him, stabbing him whenever he lowered his guard.

"Mr. Stuart? Do you need anything?"

Tristan turned to look at her, a beautiful vision even in a faded gown with a dusting rag wrapped around her locks. "You're dressed like a servant."

He hadn't meant the words to be cruel, but the flash of surprise in her eyes and the blush of shame on her cheeks told him his meaning had not come across. Tristan cleared his throat.

"Forgive me." He came to his feet. "I meant to say I find it impressive that a lady can adapt to the aftermath of war with such grace and dignity, and even dressed as one beneath her true station, she manages to remain beautiful."

The color in Miss Martin's cheeks deepened, but she did not take her gaze from him. After a moment, her eyebrows raised. "I see your skills at flattery have improved with your health."

Her voice held reprimand, yet teased at the same time, and he stared at her, unsure how he should respond. When three heartbeats passed with him incapable of formulating a reply, she spun around and slipped back into the house.

Tristan looked down at Shadow. "Well, I made a mess of that, didn't I?"

The dog cocked his head, tongue lolling out of the side of his mouth.

Now he'd started talking to a dog. He settled back down and waited again, not knowing what else he should do with himself. Mrs. Martin seemed to have no problem finding chores for him to do as soon as he'd declared himself fit. He'd been happy to put himself to the labor, earning his simple meals rather than draining the women. They had long been in need of someone to cut wood, haul water, and fix a myriad of broken things around the house, and he'd found a sense of satisfaction in being able to care for them as they had cared for him.

But even as he threw his body into his labors with vigor, the dowager's daughter seemed to look too deeply into him, sensing something ailed him even after he'd healed. Left to her, she wouldn't allow him to do anything but rest, and he loathed resting. It gave a man too much time to think.

Today the elder Martin lady was gone to town to meet with the Yankee interested in Riverbend, and he was left alone with Miss Martin, who would not allow him anything more interesting than a few dusty books. He stretched his legs and settled his back against one of the large columns that surrounded the house.

Thankfully, he'd found a suitable alternative to reading. As Mrs. Martin had readied herself to leave, he'd promised to sit out on the porch and keep watch. Not that either of them had told her about such plans. Miss Martin probably thought he merely minded her reprimands and took his leisure out of doors. In truth, his sentry duty on the porch solved the problem of leaving a young unmarried woman alone in the house with a soldier and gave the older woman peace of mind.

Shadow yawned and put his head in Tristan's lap, the sound of singing and the cool breeze lulling them both into a moment of ease. Tristan kept alert, scanning the drive and yard for any sign of trouble.

The swish of skirts had him turning his head to see Miss Martin carrying a pitcher and two glasses. She handed him one and poured yellow liquid from the pitcher into it, then did the same for herself. Her long fingers tapped the glass as she eyed him, and he realized that once again he had forgotten his manners.

"Thank you."

A small smile played on her lips, but she hid it away before it could bring its full light. "I remember when we used to have chips of ice to put into it."

He nodded and took a sip, unable to control the grimace that puckered his lips.

She laughed, a sweet sound that held not the first hint of malice. "I also remember when we had plenty of sugar." She took a sip of her own, the sourness seeming to have no effect. "I suppose I have just gotten used to things without much sugar."

Tristan took another sip, this time more prepared. "Nice to have lemons. Haven't tasted one in some time."

Miss Martin's eyes drifted down the drive. "It is one of the many blessings Mr. and Mrs. Remington bestow on us."

He followed her gaze. "You will miss them when you leave."

She eyed him, though he wasn't sure if what he'd stated had been improper or not. It seemed a fairly obvious observance.

"How do you know I will be leaving?"

He shrugged. "Heard you and your mother talking."

Miss Martin sighed. "I suppose it wouldn't be a secret."

She said it like a soldier who had come to terms with defeat. Something stirred within him, a desire to protect her from further surrender. He rolled words around in his head, choosing them carefully. "I formed the understanding that even though you would be forced to live among the enemy, your standard of living would be greatly improved…?" He watched her reaction.

She gave a small nod, and again he read resignation. "It would. And it would give Mama something fresh, which I know she desperately needs. Daddy's memory clings to the very walls here." Her eyes flicked down his borrowed clothing. "And she needs reprieve."

Tristan squeezed his hand and felt the forgotten glass, then lifted the sour liquid to his lips. He swallowed, but the stall tactic did nothing to stay the words more bitter than the drink. "A new place will not uproot the memories." The muscle in his jaw worked. "It will not dilute the pain."

She stared at him a moment, but her eyes did not hold pity. Instead, they glimmered with understanding. He felt himself relax.

"Do you miss your home?"

The words plucked at the fleeting calm her gaze had tried to instill. "I don't have a home."

Her smooth brow puckered, but before she could ask it of him, the words tumbled free. "It wasn't enough the Yanks killed my two older brothers in battle, or my father when they razed Atlanta." The words burned as they escaped his throat, desperate for release even as he hated speaking them. "But then they used my house as lodging for their officers, forcing my mother to serve them." He shook his head. "She had always been fragile. It was more than her heart could take."

Miss Martin stared at the liquid in her glass. "What will you do with your home now that the Federals are withdrawing?"

He nearly spat, but checked himself and swallowed instead. "Found out in Greenville they burned it for good measure when they departed. Accident, they say, but I know better. There's nothing to go back to now."

Her brow furrowed deeper and she drew her lower lip through her teeth. When she looked at him again, her eyes glittered with unshed tears. "I am sorry for the loss you have endured."

Tristan turned his eyes back toward the drive, unable to keep her gaze. Loss seemed an ever-present companion. A poisoned fog that hung around him, obscuring his sight of everything that lay beyond it. He squeezed his eyes shut, desperately trying to keep it from slithering deeper into his soul. He felt Miss Martin draw closer, and somewhere in the hollows of his mind he recognized her touch on his shoulder. But the air seemed to choke him even as he breathed in its clean purity.

Lord, save me from this darkness.

The unexpected prayer exploded from a tear in his soul, the first he had bothered to utter in over a year. Not since Millie....

He hung his head, knowing it too would not be answered, and then moved out of Miss Martin's grasp.

Chapter Seven

Opal clenched the fabric at her throat as though in so doing she could erase the sudden burning that took up residence there. She inhaled slowly, letting the humid air work its way down into her lungs. She knew the pain of losing a parent, but at least she still had one remaining. This poor man had lost both mother and father, as well as two brothers. She glanced down at his banded arm.

"That only makes four." The whispered words slipped past her lips, not meant to find purchase.

Mr. Stuart flinched, and Opal closed her eyes. "Forgive me. It is not my place."

He ran his calloused fingertip over the bottom black ribbon and the glint in his eyes turned cold. "The last is for Millie."

Before she could garner a response, he stepped down the porch and his long strides took him across the lawn. Opal watched him with her fingers pressed to her lips. If he continued to walk away, would he disappear from her life as quickly as he had arrived? As she'd tended him these past weeks, she'd continually done as Ella had recommended. She'd prayed he would find healing, and she prayed for wisdom to guard her heart.

Yet, still it betrayed her. Why did she feel so drawn to this man, a stranger? Why could she not let go of the foolish notion that she might find the happy end of a romantic tale? Such things did not happen during the aftermath of a devastating war. Well, except perhaps to Ella and Westley Remington. But that was different...special.

She nibbled the inside of her lip, a habit she had when she was lost in thought. Mama said it would cause wrinkles around her mouth, but she couldn't help it. Mr. Stuart came to a stop about halfway down the drive, his hands in his pockets. She tried to follow his gaze, but saw nothing. Perhaps he saw only shadows of memory. She leaned against the pillar, watching him as he fingered the fabric on his sleeve once more.

Millie. He'd said the name with such anguish that it could only belong to a lost love. The woman he had first called for when he'd opened his eyes upon her porch. Her foolish heart twisted, knowing that his own would always hold a candle for another. Opal drew herself up.

Stop this foolishness! Mr. Stuart was not some beau come to call. He was a soldier who had suffered and fought and needed her kindness. Here she stood, a silly besotted fool over the first man who stumbled upon her porch. Mama had been right. All those novels had softened her head. She was holding on to girlish hopes and weaving impossible delusions.

Help me, Lord, to be more resolute. Show me what I should do. The prayer, similar to many she'd spoken throughout the past days, sprang to mind once more as she turned away. No time to sit about woolgathering. There were chores to be completed before Mama returned from town. Perhaps with the blockade gone they might even have an early delivery of apples now that the boats ran down the river again.

Above all else, love one another, for love covers a multitude of sins. The verse manifested seemingly of its own accord and Opal paused with her hand on the doorknob. Then the rumble of carriage wheels drew her attention back toward the road, giving adequate cause to dismiss contemplating why her mind had chosen to accost her with thorny reminders that she was to love in Christian charity, not in the rendering of the heart.

She straightened her skirts and moved to aid Mama with unloading whatever supplies could be had, but it was not their pitiful mule that churned up the mud. A sleek chaise with the hood neatly folded back had paused in the drive, the proud horse secured in its harness tossing its head. Opal's stomach churned. She did not need to get a good look at the fellow in a stovepipe hat to know who had come to call.

Mr. Stuart grasped the horse's bridle and stroked its ears with his other hand. Opal moved to the top step and clasped her hands in front of her as Mama had taught. She waited for several moments, but still the men talked. What could have Mr. Stuart keeping Mr. Weir from coming on to the house? Surely idle conversation could be had in transit. In her time spent with the soldier, she had not known Mr. Stuart to be given to prolonged pleasantries. But then, perhaps they spoke of news that men folk often seemed to attempt to shield from women.

Perhaps she should see what was happening. She had no sooner taken a step in that direction when Mr. Stuart turned to her and Mr. Weir leaned forward. Both men held her in their regard, and her fingers absently moved to check her pins. Her hand brushed against the rag tied around her head to keep the dust from her hair and she quickly snatched it free.

Opal forced herself to keep her chin high even as she stuffed the cloth into her pocket and the horse resumed its prancing pace. The two wheels of the carriage sucked at the mud, slinging it up on the bright blue paint. Yesterday's rain had come in a downpour, dousing the land faster than it could be absorbed. A smirk played at the corner of her mouth. How had this dandy ridden this far south in such a frivolous conveyance? Such dainty things were meant for afternoon courtships in the park.

The thought caused her pulse to jump. He didn't come to Riverbend with any such notions, did he? She immediately chastised herself and set her teeth. She was a callow ninny, indeed! Why, to think that every man who set foot on her land had intentions of the heart....

She clenched her fist, then relaxed it and forced a placid expression to smooth her features as Mr. Weir swung down from his rig and secured the horse to the hitching post. Her gaze slid over his clean linen suit and his hat, and then back to where Mr. Stuart trudged through the damp earth. By the time her eyes swung back to Mr. Weir, he was nearly upon her.

His polished boots held none of the muck that would cling to the pair of Daddy's that Mr. Stuart wore, and as he removed his hat to offer a shallow bow, she couldn't help but notice his hair seemed as polished as his shoes.

"Good day to you, Miss Martin."

She inclined her head, but did not offer her hand. "Mr. Weir."

"Has your mother not yet returned? We spoke in town, but I did not see her on the road to the house."

Her eyes flicked to Mr. Stuart again as he came to stand at the Yankee's side. "She has not. You met with my mother?"

"Why, yes. We had a scheduled meeting." He raised his eyebrows. "She did not inform you?"

Opal scrambled for words, but it was Mr. Stuart who spoke. "Mrs. Martin has not yet returned, and as you have already spoken with her today, perhaps you should return at another time."

An annoyed glance cast over his shoulder was the only acknowledgment Mr. Weir gave the interruption. "Miss Martin, your mother agreed that I should come to the house and we would continue our discussion here. I wish to have a closer look at the grounds."

Mr. Stuart watched her carefully, but whatever thoughts played behind his eyes, he did not put them to further words. He was not a knight here to deliver her from the clutches of evil schemes, nor was Mr. Weir anything more than an opportunist who could well be the answer to Mama's prayers. The time for foolish hopes and girlhood ideals was gone. Opal drew herself to her full height and extended her arm. "Of course, sir. Do forgive my manners. It has been a long while since my mother has had gentlemen callers. Please, come in."

She opened the door for him and tried to ignore the way his eyes scrambled over every detail of both her person and the house as she gestured toward the parlor. "You can make yourself comfortable while I fetch some refreshment."

Before she could close the door, Mr. Stuart stepped inside. She hid her surprise as he hesitated in the entryway, making her lean around him to latch the door. He smelled of the soap Daddy always used, and she had to close her eyes a moment to center herself. When she opened them again, she found him watching her.

"You are welcome to sit in the parlor as well," she said, avoiding the intense eyes that tried to look too close upon her.

"If that is what you wish."

What she wished? What other reason did he have to come inside if not to continue his previous discussion with Mr. Weir? He reached out and took her hand, and her breathing stopped.

"Or I can toss him out, if you wish that instead." His voice was deep, almost a rumble from his chest.

She blinked at him, then remembered to draw air. Not a hint of mischief played in his eyes, and even though her lips parted, no words would come free. His hand still held the tips of her fingers, causing her thoughts to trip over themselves. She looked down at where the two of them touched, marveling at how such a small thing could cause her insides to unravel.

His gaze followed hers and he dropped her hand, taking a step back. When she found his eyes again, they were guarded.

"I promised your mother I would watch over you. So either I sit with him, or I send him on his way."

Opal ran her tongue over her lips to restore some of their moisture, and his gaze darted to her mouth. His eyes darkened as his shoulders expanded with a deep breath.

Feeling heat creep up her neck, she ducked her head. "If you would sit with him, I would be obliged," she muttered as she stepped around him and darted toward the safety of the empty hall. She scurried through the rear door and did not look back as she hurried toward the kitchen. Once safely ensconced inside, she let out the air contained in her lungs with a groan.

What *was* that?

Opal had little experience with men, but even she knew there had been something to the look he had given her. Confounding man! How could he look at her in such a way, when she knew he must be drowning in the loss of his Millie? She set her teeth and filled the teakettle. Mama had warned her about the desires of men. She must make sure he understood she would not be a pair of warm arms with which he could bury his loss.

She aimed to help him heal, but not like that. Her scattered thoughts jumped like frogs trying to escape a hot pan, never landing long on one thing before hopping to another. Mama must have made her final decision. Why else would she have invited Mr. Weir here? Would they like it in Massachusetts? Would she ever get to see Ella again? What would that oiled dandy do with a farm?

The thoughts peppered her, but she had answers for none of them. By the time the kettle whistled, she'd removed the last of the tea from the hidden lock box. She was loath to spend it on Mr. Weir, but Mama would be appalled if she served him bitter lemonade instead of the fine English tea Mama had gone through such pains to keep. She dumped the last of the sugar into the serving bowl, her fingers trembling as much as her heart. Nonetheless, she held her head high, and by the time she made it to the quiet parlor, she had wrapped herself in enough resolve to appear calm.

She set the serving tray on the low table and poured a cup for each of them before sitting. Thankfully, the two men had chosen the chairs flanking the settee, so she did not have to worry about sharing it with either of them. "Sugar, gentlemen?"

"After you, Miss Martin," Mr. Weir said.

Opal dipped the tip of the spoon into the white granules and dropped the miniscule amount into her cup before handing the bowl to Mr. Weir. He tilted it to the side, gathering a heaping spoonful. She glanced to Mr. Stuart, worrying there would be none left for him, but he lifted the cup to his lips and began sipping it black.

"How old are you, Miss Martin?"

Mr. Weir's question startled her, but only the clink of her spoon on the side of her teacup gave it away. "I fail to see how such information is pertinent."

Something sparked in his eyes, but it disappeared so quickly she thought she might have imagined it. "Simply making pleasant conversation."

Well, perhaps Yankees didn't find such a question rude. She tried to remind herself to remain pleasant. "I celebrated my eighteenth birthday this past December."

He nodded as though she had answered the question correctly. "Yet you remain unmarried?"

Opal truly tried not to take offense at such personal questions, but found her words tightened all the same. "As we were at war, most of the men were a bit too busy for courting."

Mr. Stuart made a funny noise in his throat that he quickly covered with a cough. Mr. Weir ignored him and waved a hand. "Of course, you are correct. How thoughtless of me."

Best turn this conversation before it became more awkward. "Did you serve in the army, Mr. Weir?" No sooner had the words left her lips than she cringed. Oh, fiddle. A Confederate and a Yank sat in her parlor and she thought *that* would make things less awkward?

But Mr. Weir merely chuckled, despite how Mr. Stuart stiffened. "Oh, no. I was far too busy to play soldier. My father is a banker, and we had business to attend." He flicked a dismissive glance at the man across from him. "Besides, I have no qualms with what you people do with your Negroes. It never bothered me a whit that you wanted to keep your slaves, so I certainly wasn't going to risk my neck shooting you over it." He grinned, but the hard look that came over Mr. Stuart's features wiped it away.

"Not all of us fought simply to keep men in chains, sir." The words were low, though said with enough ice that even Opal shivered. Mr. Stuart kept his gaze on the Yank as the baffled man cocked his head. "Some thought the government shouldn't nullify state's rights." He narrowed his eyes. "And we fought to protect our homes from invading forces that burned and pillaged."

Mr. Weir stared at him a moment, and then cleared his throat. "Yes, well, armies do squabble over territories. It is my understanding such atrocities can be attributed to both sides. It is the way of war...or so I am told." He waved a dismissive hand again, oblivious to the way color darkened the skin above Mr. Stuart's beard.

"But as I said, the war was really only fought over the South wanting to keep slaves, and the abolitionists rallying against it. I hold no grudges." He shrugged and took a sip of his tea.

Opal looked at Mr. Stuart, who clenched the teacup so tightly that she feared he might break it. He kept his gaze locked on Mr. Weir.

"It may surprise you," Mr. Stuart said, "But there were those of my household who never did understand how physical attributes made any one man less than another."

Opal pressed her fingers to her lips as Mr. Weir stared at Mr. Stuart in open confusion. Mr. Weir shifted in his seat uncomfortably and glanced at Opal, but her eyes were drawn to the conviction sparking fire in the most expressive eyes she had ever seen.

"You make a point that I have often wondered myself, Mr. Stuart," she said, keeping her lips moving even as Mr. Weir began to sputter. "For I cannot believe God would value one people over another for the mere sake of coloring."

They stared at one another for a couple of moments, more coming from Mr. Stuart's eyes than his lips. Finally, though, they curved upward, and she found the smile to say nearly as much as his eyes.

Mr. Weir laughed. "Well, if that don't beat all. And here my father warned me that I would have to encounter a bunch of angry Rebs in a swarm over losing their Negroes."

The sound of the door saved them all from what Opal was sure would have turned into an animated response from Mr. Stuart. She lurched to her feet. "Gentlemen, I believe my mother has returned."

Mr. Weir eyed Mr. Stuart as they both rose, but quickly turned his attention on Mama as she glided into the room. Mama took in the scene quickly, her eyes lingering a moment on Mr. Stuart's tight features.

"Good afternoon, Mr. Weir. I apologize for my delay, but it took longer at the postmaster than I anticipated."

"No inconvenience at all, madam. I have been taking the opportunity to get to know Miss Martin better."

Opal watched Mama closely as her gaze darted between the two of them. Why should Mr. Weir want to get to know her? Did Mama think that if she liked the man, then she would be less opposed to selling Riverbend?

Mr. Stuart spoke through clenched teeth. "If you ladies will excuse me, I aim to finish splitting some logs for the stove."

"Thank you, Mr. Stuart," Mama said, moving aside for him to pass. "Your help here has been greatly appreciated."

He uttered a reply Opal couldn't hear and then disappeared. Mama came and sat next to Opal on the settee, her gaze sliding over the now cold teakettle.

"Oh," Opal said, reaching for the pot. "Let me go warm the kettle for you so you and Mr. Weir can continue your business."

Mama laid a hand on her arm. "Oh, don't trouble yourself, dear." She glanced at Mr. Weir and then flashed a smile that seemed too tense to be genuine. "But I did get some cookies Mr. Farnsworth's wife was selling at the general store. They smelled simply divine." She stood, and Mr. Weir rose with her. "Why don't the two of you talk for a few moments while I fetch them?"

Without waiting for a reply, Mama scurried out of the room like a nervous mouse clad in widow's rags. Opal blinked a moment in surprise, then clenched her hands, realizing she had just been purposely left alone with a questionable stranger.

Chapter Eight

*T*ristan swung the axe again, hoping his emotions would flow out of his hands and splinter with the crack of the wood. How had he let himself become this tangle of useless frustrations? Sweat slipped down the nape of his neck and soured the fine shirt he had no business wearing. He lifted the blade over his head and sent it down with all the force of his anger, the snap of the log sending tremors up his arms.

First it had been worrying about Miss Martin's well-being with the inevitable loss of her home, then it had been memories of Millie, and then that infuriating codfish aristocrat with his condescension. The axe hit again, and more of his fury went out with the next log. Why had he gotten so mad in the first place? Mr. Weir held the same opinion that many men, north and south of the divide, held. If he were honest, at the start of the war he'd been just as bent on keeping slaves as the rest of them. He'd joined the army to defend his lands from invasion, but he truly believed the government had no right to tell them what they could and could not do on their own land. That had included owning people.

But all of that had changed a year ago. *Everything*

had changed a year ago. He tossed the split log aside and reached for another from the stack. What had happened with Millie and Pat had brought long-buried childhood convictions to light. Thoughts he had tried to bury and ignore.

As a boy, he never could understand *how* skin made one man better than the other, he'd just been glad he'd been born the right color. His life had been one of comforts and privilege, and theirs had been one of toil and restraint. But anyone who questioned the system received firm reprimand, so he'd learned to bury those concerns as he grew into a man.

Movement drew his attention and he caught sight of Mrs. Martin hurrying down the rear steps. Tristan paused with the axe over his head and let it come to a rest on his shoulder.

"Mr. Weir is finished with his visit already?"

Mrs. Martin paused and eyed him. "No. He is sitting with Opal."

Tristan took a step forward, his eyes darting to the closed door on the back of the house. "Alone?"

Mrs. Martin bristled and lifted her nose to look down it, but he held a height advantage over her, and she still had to raise her eyes. "Yes, but they are not entirely without a chaperone. The parlor door is open, and I am home." She flapped a bony hand at him. "It has not been so long that I have forgotten proper etiquette, Mr. Stuart."

The muscles in his jaw worked, and he hefted the axe once more. What business was it of his who these women entertained? He positioned another log on the splitting stump.

"How much longer do you intend to stay?"

He glanced up at her, unable to read the meaning behind her words. "Are you ready for me to go? I do not wish to be a burden."

"No, your help has been most welcome. You may stay on, so long as you split the wood and do the manly chores we have long been without someone to tend."

He nodded, but she still stared at him. He waited.

"But I am afraid we will be moving soon, and when that time comes, I suspect you will not wish to stay on and work for Mr. Weir."

Tristan snorted. "No, I won't be doing that."

She fiddled with her dress. "What will you be doing, then?"

"Don't know yet."

Mrs. Martin turned back toward the kitchen. "Well, when you go, be sure to take that mongrel with you."

"Shadow?"

She paused and lifted her eyebrows. "So you've named it?"

"Seemed better than calling him *dog*."

She chuckled, and Tristan found it more robust than he'd expected. "Yes, well, you shall take good care of him, and I shall be glad to be rid of him being constantly underfoot."

Tristan twirled the axe. "Odd how he would just hang around, what with no one feeding him or anything."

Her eyes widened like a child who had just been caught stealing candy. Then she narrowed her gaze.

"Well, I couldn't very well leave a pitiful creature to die on my porch, now could I?"

A smile tugged his lips. "I am sure Shadow will forever be grateful for your charity, ma'am."

She mumbled something and hurried on to the kitchen, only to emerge a few moments later with a small package. Without a word, she untied the string, fetched a delicate confection from inside and held it out to him.

He took it without hesitation, the scent of sweetness already tickling his nose. "Thank you."

"Yes, well, best you keep up your strength. I need you to fix the hinge on the mule's stall before you put him in for the night."

Tristan watched her disappear inside, and then sat to savor the treat.

Opal rubbed a loose thread between her fingers, trying to find a topic of conversation that might refocus Mr. Weir's steady gaze. What could she say that would please Mama? Did she think Opal could butter him up in hopes of him offering a higher price?

"You are quite lovely. Appealing in a simple sort of way."

Opal looked up. He seemed to mean it as a compliment. "Did you know that my father commissioned a French craftsman from New Orleans to carve the moldings?"

He blinked. "Your mother mentioned it."

"And the table in the dining room, it would stay with the house. It is a fine piece of craftsmanship."

The corners of his mouth pulled down. "I'm sure. But enough about the house. Tell me something about you. What do you enjoy?"

Ignoring the squirm in her stomach, Opal glanced at the door. What took Mama so long? "Oh, well, I like to read."

He made a startled noise, drawing her gaze back to his smooth face. "Oh, well. I meant something...more appropriate. Something useful."

She cocked her head. "Useful? Well, I have managed the daily tasks at the house and have become more proficient in cooking, though I confess I am still not all that adept with a needle. But you asked for things I enjoy. I enjoy the opera, though I've no more occasions to go, and reading."

Mr. Weir's eyes lit. "The opera. We shall take in a show, then."

"Pardon?" Where did this man think he would be able to see an opera in Mississippi? And for that matter, his assumption that she would accompany him was audacious.

"Do you enjoy the theater as well? I am sure we will be able to take in several during the summers."

Opal considered her words. "Mr. Weir, I am afraid I do not understand."

He leaned forward. "Your mother did not mention my proposal?"

"Pro...proposal?" She nearly choked on the word.

He smiled. "Ah, well, forgive me. I suppose that

does take some of the heart out of the business. I have offered to take you on as my wife. I'll expect you to maintain the household, and I will restore you to your previous standard of living."

She gaped at him, no words finding purchase upon her lips. He began a tumult of words that she couldn't grasp, her mind still reeling. He didn't seem to notice, and by the time Mama stepped into the room, he'd rambled an entire monologue.

"Mrs. Martin," Mr. Weir said, coming to his feet at her entrance. "Your daughter and I were just discussing plans for the future."

Mama looked at Opal, then she shook her head. "Mr. Weir, I believe you have taken my daughter by surprise. I said we could discuss courtship *after* we come to a settlement about the house."

Heat seared its way up from Opal's stomach and burned the back of her throat. She rose. "If you two will excuse me, I'm afraid I am not feeling well."

Mr. Weir sputtered something, but Mama's words stayed him. "Certainly, dear. Take a few moments to get some fresh air while I finish the visit with our guest."

Mama's tone held apology, but Opal's head spun too quickly for her to try to return Mama's gaze. She grasped the parlor doorframe for support. The rear door offered a beacon of hope and she scrambled to it, glad to escape the confines of the house. The sky had darkened, giving the early afternoon the look of evening. Even still, it felt brighter than the suffocating panic in the parlor. A cool breeze brushed her cheeks as she closed the door behind her.

The dog greeted her with the thump of its tail. She moved to shoo him away, but then thought better of it. This creature had never offered anything more than a happy canine expression and a friendly nature. With a sigh, she bent and patted him on the head.

"And what are we to do with you when we leave?"

"Mrs. Martin says he is to go with me."

Opal startled at Mr. Stuart's voice, but hid it. "That is well and good." She gave the dog another pat and then straightened, unsure what to do with herself under his heavy gaze.

Mr. Stuart scratched the back of his neck. "Things go all right in there?"

His shirt clung to his chest, the damp fabric finding every hardened muscle. Opal averted her gaze. How different he looked than the smooth Mr. Weir. "He and Mama are discussing things, though I wish they would just hurry up and settle on a price. He wants to buy, she wants to sell. Let us have done."

He took a step closer, the axe he carried slung over his broad shoulder. His deep brown gaze assessed her, asking questions his lips didn't need to form.

"I...I suppose I will be moving to Massachusetts to live with Mama's cousin." She successfully kept a hitch from her voice, unable to mention the other option Mama seemed to be considering. "It will be much nicer than living here, hoping we can survive the winter."

"I suppose." He continued to stare at her.

"And where will you go, Mr. Stuart?" she asked, scrambling for something more to say. Something that would keep him in her presence a moment longer, if for nothing more than the foolishness of her hopeless heart.

"Tristan." He held her gaze, as though waiting for her to acknowledge the invitation before he would answer her question.

"Where will you go, Tristan?"

Something sparked in his eyes, but she didn't dare contemplate its meaning. "I don't know. West, maybe."

She'd heard of people heading toward the western coast, trying to set up new lives for themselves away from the war. "A good plan."

He lifted the axe from his shoulder and let it come to rest at his side. "What's the banker going to do with Riverbend?"

She barked a bitter laugh. "For some reason he has this notion that I would stay on as his wife and run his household, and perhaps manage the plantation, though I cannot fathom where he concocted such an idea. As for farming, well, I don't see him having much of a hand with that, so who is to say what will become of this place?"

Tristan's eyes darkened. "You are not considering his marriage offer, are you?"

She spread her hands. "I suppose any normal lady would be glad to see her former lifestyle of plenty restored and would be glad to wed an attractive young man with substantial wealth. Many young ladies spend their society years clamoring for such a match."

He dropped the axe and took the steps, coming to stand only an arm's length in front of her.

"But...perhaps I am not...a normal lady." The words came out breathy as she tilted her head back to look at him.

Slowly, he reached out a hand and took hold of a lock of her hair, rubbing it between his fingers. "I daresay that is truth, Miss Martin."

"Opal."

Tristan stepped closer. "Opal." He dropped the hair and traced a finger along her jaw. "Not a normal lady at all. Far better, I say. With more compassion, grace, and kindness than that scoundrel deserves."

She blinked up at him as he leaned closer, her breath snagging in her chest. The world seemed to slow, each pump of her heart sending heat through her veins. He cupped her cheek in his hand, then his lids lowered as he rested his forehead against hers.

"And Lord forgive me, far better than this broken soul could ever hope for." His whispered words brushed against her lips just before he lowered his mouth to hers.

In a sweep of emotion she pressed her lips back into his, feeling the tingle of his whiskers against her face. For one intoxicating moment he held there, and then stepped away, hanging his head.

"Forgive me. I should have never taken such a liberty." The haunted look in his eyes returned, and he turned away.

Overhead, the crack of thunder split the sky, causing her to jump. She placed her fingers to her lips as though that would hold the sensation of his kiss in place. Then she watched as he stalked out into the gathering storm.

It started as a trickle, just a dusting of moisture that pulled some of the heat from his skin, but in the few moments it took Tristan to get across the rear lawn, the rain gathered and now fell with devilish intensity. He shook his head, shortened locks sending a spray of droplets to join their fellows.

He shouldn't be standing here in the rain like a fool, but neither could he return to the house. What had possessed him to take Miss Martin into his embrace? To sully lips that he would guess had never known a man's touch before? The lasting sensation of her sent another wave of heat through his center, further knocking him off balance. Something in that fleeting moment of sweet pleasure had unmoored him and sent him into unrelenting waves of uncertainty.

Tristan pressed the heel of his hand into his eye. Why did he have to open somewhere in his depths that he could never close again? The familiar ache, the crushing sorrow that had been his daily companion, pressed down upon him again, reminding him that he had been foolish to think the reprieve he'd found here could last. He'd been delusional to think he could stay here and not taint anyone. To taste of purity and not ruin it. His gaze fell upon the river, its murky waters gulping up the rain and churning with as much intensity as the fire in his chest.

He clutched at his shirt, desperately wanting it to relent, to leave him be, even if in so doing he remained only a shell. But he deserved no such mercy. Not he who had owned men like chattel. And then robbed other men of their lives when they tried to stop him. He had broken many of God's commandments. He had not honored his mother, and stayed at her side. He had stolen supplies from the enemy. He had killed men in battle. Had watched their lifeblood drain out with detached indifference.

Forgive me, God. It is another failure, another weakness. Though I do not deserve it, save me from this darkness that consumes me. Send me something of your light. Show me you have not forgotten me, for once I was yours.

"Tristan!"

He turned, unsure if the call of his name had sprung from his own desperation or from lips that should not be so near. Through the sheets of falling rain, a flash of color drifted through the haze. Opal held the bunched fabric of her skirts in her hands, her booted feet slipping in the mud as she struggled to get to him.

In two strides, he had her by the elbow. Water streamed down her face and clung to her lashes like tiny diamonds. She shouldn't be here.

"What are you doing?"

The bite of his words didn't send her running as it should. Instead, she turned her chin up, the defiant set to her jaw warning him a scolding was forthcoming. It was no less than he deserved.

"I'm saving you!" She grasped his forearms, her wide eyes a mixture of fear and anger.

"What?"

She flung a hand at the river. "I'll not let you go in again! I swear I will not!"

He turned to look at the churning waters lapping at the edges of the bank. He scowled. It had risen at least eight inches since he last looked upon it. He glanced back to the house, situated far too near.

He started pulling on Opal's arms. "Come, Miss Martin, let's get you back inside."

She planted her heels. "You must let go of some of this pain, or it is going to steal from you all that remains of life."

A growl rumbled in his chest, but she only stepped closer, defying him. Did she not see the danger she was in? The concern in her eyes softened his edges of steel, robbing them of the cuts they should deliver.

He gentled his tone. "This is hardly the place for such a conversation."

"If I leave you alone, I fear you may do something foolish. And if I take you into the house, this moment will be gone and you will never speak of what happened."

"You want me to speak of it?" How could he? How could he voice things that would only douse the guarded affection he'd glimpsed in her eyes and replace it with the hatred he deserved?

She reached up and placed a hand on his cheek, and he longed to hold her again. Tristan shoved the sentiment aside. He was a sinking ship, and she should not go down with him. Better he undo this now before it became more than he could bear.

He grabbed her sodden elbow and thrust her toward the house. She nearly lost her balance, but he kept her upright, hauling her away from the rising river. "What would you have me say? I am sorry I took liberties that were not mine." He pulled her through the mud, heedless of the way it sucked at his boots. "I should never have stolen that from you. It was a mistake. You have my word it will never happen again."

"But, but…I…." She tried to stall his progress, but he kept his grip firm and his pace steady. "I'm not going to marry him!" She yanked her arm free, slipping and falling to the ground.

"You'll go north," he said through gritted teeth, thrusting his hands into the mud and underneath her. Tristan set his feet and lifted her from the ground. "And you will forget about that rascal. And you will forget about me. Live a better life."

She gasped and snaked her arm around his neck. "I cannot forget about you." The words, spoken so close to his ear, twisted his gut.

"You must."

Her fingers dug into his shoulder and then retreated as he hauled her up onto the porch and set her on her feet.

"Of course." She lowered her head, a vibrant flower withering underneath all that soiled him. "There will always be Millie."

He froze. What did Millie have to do with this? "What?"

"I know you will always love her, but I thought…that maybe…" her voice crumbled and she put her fist to her mouth. "I am a fool."

Water coursed down her cheeks, and he knew tears mingled with the rain. Tears *he* had caused. He clenched his hands. When he could not form words through the constriction in his throat, she gave a sob and darted into the house, leaving him alone with his shattered thoughts.

Chapter Nine

Opal burst into the house in a sodden heap of mud and dejection. She dripped upon the floor she had just scrubbed, clods of ruddy clay clinging to her hem. Why? Why must she always hold on to hope when doing so only led her to pain? Hope the war wouldn't come, hope Daddy would return home, hope that there would be a light in this endless swarm of loss and misery.

All of it pointless.

"Opal!" Mama screeched, hurrying toward her. "What has happened?"

"The storm…." As though in confirmation of her words, the house shook with a crack of thunder.

"And you went out in it?" Mama stopped in front of her, fingers working at the fabric at the base of her throat. "Did you fall?"

Opal merely bobbed her head. "I'm sorry."

"Well, now, let's just get you cleaned up. I'll have Mr. Stuart stoke a fire and get some water heated for you for a bath."

He was likely already gone, but she didn't have the energy to say so.

"What's this?" Mr. Weir appeared out from the parlor, his eyes growing wide.

"Why is he still here?" Opal whispered through clenched teeth.

Mama turned her back to the carpetbagger, hiding some of Opal's condition behind her own frame. "I couldn't send him on his way in the storm. That would be ill-mannered."

Opal began to sputter, but then clenched her teeth even tighter. What did it matter anyway? She moved to step around Mama and head toward the stairs, trying to hold on to at least a fraction of her dignity.

"Miss Martin, is this sort of behavior common for you?" The corners of Mr. Weir's mouth bent under the weight of his disapproval.

Did she normally go about sliding in the mud like a pig in its sty? Anger boiled in her stomach, released in the snap of a single word. "No."

He seemed relieved, falling in step beside her as she tromped to the stairs. "Good then. I can't have my wife acting in such an inappropriate manner. It is my hope that I will eventually be able to take you to Washington."

Opal jerked to a halt. "Excuse me?"

The smile that twisted his lips looked equal parts condescending and placating. "I'm sure there are things that women do out here in the country that seem normal to you, but understand those things wouldn't be acceptable in fine society. But don't worry, I will teach you." His voice deepened, and his lecherous gaze roaming over the sodden dress clinging to her every curve caused her insides to constrict. "Indeed, I have *lots of things* to teach you."

Standing in a ruined dress, her heart raw and her senses flailing, Opal couldn't bring herself to proffer politeness, nor could she hide her true thoughts any longer. She took a step toward him, her pulse pounding. Somewhere in the peripheral of her senses, she heard Mama's gasp, heard her speak something, but Opal ignored her.

"Let us make one thing very clear. I will *never* consent to marry a greedy opportunist like you. I'll not be your housekeeper or your pet." Her rage gathered with every word, and she stepped closer to him, poking him in the chest.

He gaped at her, his complexion reddening with every breath he drew through his pointy nose. Something dangerous sparked in his eyes, warning her not to press further. But the words were already sharpened on her tongue and flew out to flay him.

"And I will *never* warm your bed!"

His nostril's flared, and in that moment, the mask of the friendly, simple dandy fell away. His eyes bulged and before she could step back, he grabbed her arm.

"How *dare* you speak to me that way, you wretched little urchin."

Mama yelped. "Unhand her!"

Mr. Weir hauled Opal against him, his eyes boring into hers. "You will do everything I tell you to do, or I will see to it that you and your vexatious mother are left to beg for scraps."

Opal struggled to free herself from his grasp, but

he sank his fingers into her skin. Mama pulled at his arm, begging for him to let her go. Mr. Weir simply swung out his free arm and batted her away as though Mama were nothing more than an irksome fly.

He sneered. "Now, I grow tired of these games."

"Please, just give us the money for the house and we will be gone from here."

Opal had never heard such terror in her mother's voice, and it turned her blood cold.

Mr. Weir glanced at her, and then as suddenly as he had turned into a terror, the fire drained from his eyes and he dropped Opal's arm. She rubbed at the sore place, biting her lip.

He shook his head. "Now why did you have to go and make me do that?"

She swallowed hard, glancing at Mama. Mama had gone completely pale, and looked as though she were about to faint. Opal took a small step back. This man was dangerous.

"Forgive me," she squeaked, trying to find a modicum of strength to free them from this madman's wrath. "I...I was merely distraught after falling in the mud, and humiliated that you had to see me in such a despicable state. I...didn't mean it." Her voice quivered, but it only seemed to help him swallow the words.

He sighed. "I understand. But we will not let ourselves get in the mud again, now will we?"

She shook her head, grasping the stair rail.

"That's good then. And I shall forgive you this once for speaking to me in such a manner. But now we know not to speak that way *ever again*, don't we?"

Opal lowered her eyes. "Yes."

He placed a finger under her chin and forced her to look at him. "Do not fret, I said I forgive you. We can put it behind us now."

She held his gaze, afraid to breathe until he finally removed his touch.

His eyes roamed down her dress. "You need to throw that one away."

"All right."

He smiled, his shoulders relaxing. "There now. See, isn't that better?"

She stared at him, willing her features to remain smooth even as he took a step closer, only a hand's breadth away. "How about I find you another gown? Something more fitting for you to be seen with me in?"

"I..." She glanced at Mama, who had begun fanning herself. "That would be lovely. Thank you."

He reached up and grasped her shoulder, and it took all of her willpower not to flinch. "I must tend to some business, but it shouldn't take long. When I return, I expect your mother to have her affairs in order and her things packed. You should prepare yourself for the wedding and be sure the master chamber is in order. Once we have said our vows, we will send Mrs. Martin off with a stipend and a train ticket to Massachusetts."

Opal pressed her lips together and gave a small nod. He squeezed her shoulder and then stepped back. "Good. Then I shall see you again soon, my dear."

Without bothering to bid Mama goodbye, he fetched his hat and opened the front door. The rain had slackened to a drizzle, and though he cursed it, he stepped out of the house. As soon as the door latch clicked, Mama scurried to it and turned the lock.

Then she collapsed into a heap on the floor.

Chapter Ten

*T*ristan watched the swirl of the river as it tested its confines, and then shook off the chains of its banks. It crept tentatively at first, caressing the grass with gentle exploration. Then it became greedy, gathering up its brethren falling from the sky and building its ranks.

He took a step back, and then another. The river would swell, and do what it had always done. The river was not like men. It could not be contained, or broken. It could do only what nature, what God himself, had commissioned for it to do. It did not fail, it did not sin, and it did not carry a conscience for its destruction.

But Tristan did.

Forgive me.

The water lapped his boots, causing him to retreat. He didn't dare look at the house, which sequestered Opal from him. What did she do now? Did she see how hopeless he was? Did she now realize that even a slimy blowhard was a more favorable option than...?

He shivered. Than what? Him? When had he even begun to let himself think that would be an option? He deserved no such goodness in his life. Not after the man he had been, or the things he had done in war. He should have defied his father's wishes and freed his family's slaves when he had the chance. But he had been too set in the old ways…a coward.

If he had done things differently, then Millie would have never tried to help Pat run. Then she would have never been out there…alone….

Pain constricted in his chest. He should have been there. He should have put his own foolish pride aside and done what was right. Millie had paid a high price for his stubbornness. Rain coursed through his hair, washing the scar that remained from an injury he didn't even remember receiving. He only remembered finding out about the loss of his home and then waking up with more pain.

Pain that Opal had tried to bind, just as her gentle sweetness had tried to wash and bind the pain in his heart. He turned to look at the house and, for a moment, wondered if he could ever throw aside the past and start anew. Could he find redemption in saving Riverbend and dedicating his life to the woman who saw into his darkness and still reached for him?

But he could never offer her this battered heart or a shell of a man too heavy-laden with all he had done and all he had lost to ever be whole again.

Come unto me, all ye that labor and are heavy laden.

The thought pressed itself upon him, and he drew a quick breath. He looked around, but no sounds greeted him beyond the rush of water and the steady pelt of rain that obstructed his vision and clouded his senses.

I will give you rest.

He didn't deserve rest. He didn't deserve happiness. He didn't deserve anything more than to let the waters sweep him away. Water dripped from his lashes and mingled with the moisture pricking his eyes.

For the wages of sin is death.

Pain lanced through him, as sharp and sure as shrapnel. Tristan had sinned in abundance. He deserved the river, even as now it came for him, sucking at his ankles and twisting itself around his feet.

Christ also suffered for us....who bore our sins in his own body on the tree...by whose stripes ye were healed. As far as the east is from the west, so far hath he removed our transgressions from us. God's mercy is the cause, the removal of sin the result.

Where did these verses, so long buried in his soul, come from? He had not set himself to memorizing them and had not laid eyes upon scripture since he left for war.

He'd been young when he'd asked the reverend to pray for him; a youth who did not understand what it meant to offer himself in service. He had accepted the gift of salvation, but had failed in aligning himself under orders.

He'd been glad for the gift, but hadn't really wanted to surrender to the giver. And where had that gotten him? It had taken him far from the light, a light he now could barely remember. Tristan hung his head. He had wandered, but he could not, *would* not, let the darkness take him.

Therefore if any man be in Christ, he is a new creature: the old things are passed away; behold, all things become new.

New. He did not have to be the youth consumed

with pride. He did not have to be a soldier doused in misery. He did not have to be a ghost of misfortune set to float through the world and never live in it again.

Tristan lifted his face to the cleansing rain, feeling a great weight lift from him even as the river pulled at him. He'd asked for forgiveness, and it had been granted. He was made new. It was time he started acting like it.

The waters surged, tugging on his legs and pulling him off balance. Had he waded into the river? Tristan blinked, coming out of his stupor.

The river!

It had swept out of its banks, through the yard, and now lapped at the foundation of the house! Water wrapped itself around his waist, trying to unmoor him. Any moment, it would push up onto the porch and seize the house. He had to get inside and warn the women. He set his feet into motion, each step causing his muscles to strain.

"Tristan!"

He looked up, hoping he had only imagined the panicked voice. "Opal! Do not leave the porch—"

She clutched a column, her face a mask of fear. "Tristan! It is Mama!"

He set his teeth and tried to move faster, but it took all of his effort to keep his feet underneath him in the churn of the water. It surged, pushing against his back. He stumbled.

"Tristan!"

He thrust his arms out to his sides, regaining his footing. Now, if he could only get….

Opal screamed.

In a flash of fabric and flailing arms, Opal's skirts caught the current like a sail in the wind. She dipped beneath the surface of the muddy water, and he lunged. The swollen river snaked around him, seeming as desperate to keep him from his destination as he was to obtain it. He fought against the force of the current, struggling to get to the house even as the water strained to carry him away from it. He kicked his feet, trying to reach where she had gone under just off the porch.

Eddies swirled, and the water lapped at the house, but he saw no sign of Opal. He twisted, frantically seeking a splash of yellow fabric or a splay of cinnamon hair. How could she have disappeared that quickly?

There!

Her head bobbed up again and she sputtered, just out of reach. Tristan lunged away from the house, letting the desires of the current pull him toward her. "Opal!"

Tristan reached, his fingers grasping at fabric, but slipping free. She swept farther away, the river taking her with it as it galloped across the yard. If he didn't reach her before the water struck the woods....

He pumped his arms, slicing his body through the water. Something struck his back, sending a surge of pain down his spine. Still he kicked, fighting water more furiously than he ever had the enemy, until he finally grasped a handful of fabric. He gave a mighty yank and snatched her body toward him.

Opal screamed, but the terrified sound was choked off and dissolved into a spasm of coughs. She threw her arms wildly, smacking him and making it difficult to get a hold on her.

"Stop!"

She paid no heed to his command and continued to fight against the waters. She coughed, and then slipped beneath the surface. His arm shot out and wrapped around her, and he pulled backward. She broke the surface, sputtering, and then went limp.

Tristan pulled her against him, setting her head against his shoulder. Her body floated up to the surface, the water splaying her skirts like a yellow ribbon on a canvas of muddy brown. Tristan groaned and began to swim backward, hampered by her weight and having the use of only one arm.

He kicked and fought against the current, a desperate battle against a foe that never wearied. Moment by moment, and inch by inch, Tristan hauled her back toward the house. He would not let the river take them.

Behind him, Shadow barked frantically. Fatigue pulled at him, his muscles burning. Still Tristan fought until his shoulders hit against something solid. Praise the Lord! He'd reached the house. He turned, thankful that he could get his feet underneath him this close to the foundation. He shifted his body, using the waist-high bricks of the house to keep him steady as he struggled to lift Opal to safety.

She groaned as he hefted her head and shoulders up onto the safety of the rear porch. Then he braced himself against the bricks and set his feet against the tug of the water. Ignoring the burning and trembling muscles in his arms, he slowly worked the rest of her body out of the river. Then with what little strength still clung to him, Tristan hauled himself out of the water and crumpled beside her, heaving.

Opal turned her head, her chest burning. Her lungs heaved, bringing up a mouthful of dirty water. She coughed, then inhaled a blissful breath of air. She gulped it in, thankful to be free of the waters. With a groan, she rolled to the other side, finding Tristan beside her.

Alarmed, she bolted up and grabbed his shoulders, flinging him onto his back.

"Tristan!"

His eyes popped open, and she let out a protracted breath. He was alive.

She remained leaning over him, her hands pressed into his shoulders and her face hovering above his. He studied her, and something about his eyes seemed…different. She leaned closer, and he grinned.

"Are you going to kiss me?"

She gasped and leaned back, but didn't move away. "What a thing to say!"

He chuckled. "Seems a fitting reward for saving your life."

Opal blinked at him a moment, then allowed an impish turn of her mouth. "Is that so?"

Tristan started to nod, then his forehead crinkled and the playfulness left his gaze. "Why did you get in the water?"

Heat crept up her neck. "I saw you start to fall and…." Her heart lurched. "Oh! We have to get Mama!"

She struggled to her feet, her dress a heavy mass of soggy fabric. Tristan mumbled something, but seemed to be gaining his legs as well. Opal glanced behind her, amazed that the river now flowed at the very edges of her home. She sucked a breath, and with it released a prayer. "Don't let it take us."

A hand settled on her shoulder, and she looked up into Tristan's tired face.

"You shouldn't have tried to jump in for me. Can you even swim?"

She bit her lip and shook her head. It had been foolish. She hadn't even been thinking. "Mama has fainted. I need your help."

He followed her inside, the two of them leaving trails of water and mud like oversized slugs. Mama lay right where Opal had left her at the front door. She scrambled over to her and lifted Mama's head, relieved she breathed slow and easy.

"Mama?"

Mama remained still even as Tristan put his arms under her and lifted, his face revealing some of the strain he obviously tried to hide. He puffed out his cheeks and hauled Mama into the parlor, gently setting her on the settee.

"What happened?"

Opal twisted her fingers. "She just fainted, and fell to the floor. I fear she may have bumped her head."

Tristan stood there dripping on the floor, watching

her. "What happened to Mr. Weir?"

"I...." She glanced toward the window. "I don't know. He left, Mama fainted, and I came to get you...."

Tristan followed her gaze. "He left during this storm?"

She nodded. "I do hope he didn't get caught in the waters." And she did. No matter what kind of scoundrel he was, she didn't wish for him to come to harm. She merely wished for him to leave her and Mama alone. But at the same time, it was a pity, since now he expected her to marry him and would soon return. She just hoped she could keep him at bay when he did.

"Go and get yourself into something dry. I will sit with her until you return."

Opal nearly refused, but something about accepting the gentle offer of his aid seemed right. Mama should awaken soon, but if she didn't, Opal would send Tristan to fetch Sibby. The intrepid woman always seemed to have something to help. Opal whispered her thanks, cast Mama another glance, and then hurried from the room.

Chapter Eleven

*T*ristan looked down at the woman on the small couch, amused when her eyes flew open as soon as Opal scrambled from the room.

"I knew you were not asleep."

The dowager sniffled and pushed herself into a sitting position, somehow still managing to look refined even under the circumstances. "Nonsense. I have just this moment regained my senses." She glanced at him, a small spark of worry in her faded eyes. "I take it I succumbed to the flutters?"

"That would be my assumption, ma'am, as you were unconscious on the floor."

She lowered her eyes to study her clasped hands. In the time he had spent here, he had not seen Mrs. Martin look this subdued.

He scratched the wet hair at the back of his scalp. "If I may ask, did something happen to upset you?"

She looked up at him, studying him as though to assess whether or not she found him worthy of an explanation. Then she angled her chin toward one of the chairs flanking the settee. "Sit, Mr. Stuart, if you please."

"I cannot, for as you can see, in my current state, I would ruin your furniture."

She glanced down at his clothes, as though just now noticing he dripped from crown to boot. "I do not wish to unduly burden you, but since I am not blind to the way you look at my daughter, I feel you should have the right to know."

Unease settled in his stomach, and he clenched his fists at his sides.

"Mr. Weir has declared he will marry Opal and send me away with a stipend and a train ticket. He aims to pry Riverbend from us."

He'd expected an underhanded deal from the carpetbagger, but…. "You mean he thinks to gain the house by marriage, rather than purchasing it as he said?"

Mrs. Martin nodded.

"Opal mentioned you and he had entered into a discussion about a marriage arrangement."

Mrs. Martin scoffed, making a rather unladylike sound from the back of her throat. "Don't be absurd, sir. I merely said I would entertain the discussion for courtship after he agreed on my price for the house." She lowered her eyes. "It was only meant to be a tactic to get him to agree to a more favorable price. I never intended for that miscreant to make a claim on my daughter."

Tristan's jaw clenched. "And what does Miss Martin think of the proposal?"

Mrs. Martin stared at him. "Surely you do not need to ask such a thing. I assure you, I will not allow her to marry that man in exchange for the money he provides.

I do not think he will treat her in a gentlemanly manner."

Despite himself, Tristan's shoulders relaxed. Before he could talk himself out of it, he blurted, "What about me?"

The corner of Mrs. Martin's mouth twitched. "What *about* you?"

"Well, I...."

"Yes? Do you have intentions you wish to speak to me before she returns?"

Tristan glanced at the door. "War took a great deal from me, and though the Lord is merciful, I fear the horrors will visit me for a long time to come."

"I believe this entire country will suffer such a fate with you, dear boy. Best we learn to deal with it together."

He couldn't be sure, but it seemed an acceptance of his struggles, and perhaps a blessing upon the question he longed to ask. He cleared his throat. "Mrs. Martin, would you accept my intentions to court, and eventually wed, your daughter, if she will have me?"

Mrs. Martin made a point of studying him over-long, but he kept his gaze steady under her regard.

"And what of Riverbend? You have seen her attachment to it."

"I have the money I put away from my time in the army, as well as what remains of my family's estate. It isn't what it once was, but my father was wise in his finances." He couldn't help but chuckle. "And to think I once considered it unpatriotic of him to keep a portion of his money in Northern banks instead of turning it all into worthless Confederate currency. It would be my honor to care for the two women whom I hold great affection for."

She stared at him a few moments longer, a smile belying the shimmer of tears in her eyes. "Then you have my blessing."

"Blessing?" Opal's voice danced into the room. "Blessing for what?"

Tristan whirled around. "We were...." He hesitated. "Why are you dressed in mourning?"

Opal glanced down at her dress, her cheeks turning a fetching shade of pink. She had twisted her damp locks up into a braid that wrapped around her head, and even in blacks, she looked fetching.

"It was the only one I had that was...clean." She looked to her mother. "Are you feeling better, Mama?"

"I am, dear. Quite better, in fact." She looked back at Tristan, who shifted his feet. Drat! Why must he feel like a new recruit under the assessing eye of a commanding officer?

Tristan looked down at his wet clothes and the dark place he'd made on the rug. "If you ladies will please excuse me, I am in need of a fresh set of clothing."

Opal crossed her arms. "Is there anything you wish to tell me?"

Mama smirked. "If you see Mr. Weir on our land again, shoot him."

"Mama!"

She waved her hand. "What?" When Opal made a face, she laughed. "Oh, fine. You may shoot *at* him, but you don't have to wound him. The crack of gunfire should do enough to get his attention and get through to him that we will not allow him on our property again."

Opal bit her lip. "I cannot marry him, Mama."

"Ha! Of course not, child. Do you think me daft? I'll not have my daughter in the hands of that monster."

Relief swept through her even as she asked, "But what of Riverbend, and your new life in Massachusetts?"

"Never you mind that."

Opal resisted the urge to glance behind her, in the direction Tristan had gone. They had other pressing matters. "The river flooded, Mama. I am surprised it has not yet breeched the house."

Mama jumped to her feet. "What!" In a flash of black cotton, she dashed toward the rear door and flung it open. The waters flowed through the yard, a swift current that beat upon the kitchen, no doubt ruining everything they had not stored on an upper shelf.

Mama put her hand to her lips and gave a muffled cry. "It will all be ruined."

Footsteps sounded from behind and Tristan came to stand by them, watching the waters rush past. The rain had stopped, and the clouds had lightened to a dull gray.

"A miracle it didn't rise over the porch," Tristan said.

They watched the river sweep by in a display of power only a force of nature could perform. After a few more moments, Mama declared she needed a rest, and disappeared into the house.

Opal and Tristan continued to watch, time slipping away. Finally, the water slowed in its devilish rush, and it seemed they were free from the danger of the river claiming the house. They had been spared.

Thank you, Lord.

"That water nearly took me away," Opal whispered.

"Me, too," Tristan said, his eyes focused ahead.

"Thank you for coming after me. I meant to come for you, but instead almost got us both drowned."

He turned, and she could feel his gaze on her. That feeling, the one Ella had described, took up residence in every thud of her heart. But was it merely a hope that something akin to the romance in storybooks existed? Or, at the very least, a more blissful alternative than the kind of life Mr. Weir represented?

"What happened to Millie?" She hadn't meant to ask, but then, she needed to know. Perhaps the truth would shake her free of these odd feelings and give her the strength to face whatever tomorrow might bring.

Tristan sighed, and his shoulders slumped. "She died. I wasn't there to protect her."

Opal waited, wondering if he would explain more. But after he remained silent for several moments, she finally decided it wasn't a memory he wished her to be a part of. She gazed back over the thrashing waters, reminding herself that she'd been blessed beyond measure. They had likely lost most of their supplies in the kitchen, but the house had escaped the river's wrath.

For now, that would be enough.

"It was my fault."

Tristan's voice startled her. She glanced at his profile, noting the hard set to his jaw.

"Millie always said slavery was wrong," he said, flexing his fingers at his side as though they itched to reach out for something. "Even at a young age, she defied both her elders and her social standing and spoke against it at every opportunity. The war only made her more outspoken. When my father died, she begged me to free our slaves."

Our....

Had she been not only his love, but his wife? Opal let this new truth settle over her. Of course, it would make sense. And why should it make a difference?

He cleared his throat, as though it constricted against his words. Opal wrapped her arms around herself, not sure she wanted to hear more.

"But I was a coward. I told her we would win this war, and then I would decide their fate on my own terms." He looked at her, his eyes clouded in the waning light. "It shouldn't have even been my decision. But...I was the only one left."

"Your fathers and your brothers?"

"Dead," Tristan said, his Adam's apple bobbing. "And Mother's health was already failing by then. I begged Millie to stop speaking out. She was gaining attention. I told her just to wait until I came home, and we would devise a suitable solution."

He looked back out over the waters. "That wasn't good enough for Millie. When I returned to the battlefield after a short furlough to mourn my father and brothers, she started taking drastic action. Mother was too sick by then to do much to stop her." The look in his eyes turned haunted again.

"You don't have to tell me if it causes you pain."

"No, it is a wound that needs to be lanced. I cannot heal if I refuse to let the pain out."

Opal turned her gaze back to the lawn, giving him the time he needed. The birds tentatively started their songs once more in the gathering dusk, brought on all the earlier by the cloud cover. The thick scent of rain permeated the air, and drops fell from branches, swallowed up by the rushing sound of the misplaced river.

Beyond where they stood, the water had dipped lower on the stairs, now leaving the topmost step uncovered. Hopefully, the waters would continue to recede and leave them in peace.

"Millie escorted slaves in small bands through the woods," Tristan said, his voice hard. "She was helping them to a meeting point where they could be taken to another route to escape to the North. Somehow, she must have been discovered." He sighed, the telling seeming to weary him as much as the waters had. "Discovered by the kind of men who didn't take too kindly to such things, even though it was none of their business."

Opal's throat tightened, and she clenched the fabric of her skirt, its color now seeming appropriate for this day.

Tristan's voice grew deeper, and his words came out at a growl. "That night, she took her maid, Pat, a girl she had been fond of her entire life, and another young woman who was swollen with child."

Opal reached out and placed her hand on his sleeve, aching for the pain that radiated in his voice.

"She was so young, Opal. Barely seventeen. A sweet child that had always been a light to our lives. The things those men did to those girls…." His voice caught and he hung his head.

Overcome, Opal slipped her arm around his waist and pulled herself against him. It was meant in comfort, the only means by which she could think to offer it. "I'm deeply sorry for the loss of your family, and for the pain caused to your wife."

He shifted underneath her grasp, but she didn't look up at him.

"My wife?"

Heat crept up her neck. That is what he'd said…right? She picked through her memories. No, he'd never actually said anything of the sort. She'd merely assumed. "Millie…she wasn't your wife?"

He took her by the shoulders and turned her to face him. "Millie was my sister. Stolen from us and abused because she believed differently than people thought she was supposed to. When did I ever say anything to make you think otherwise?"

Embarrassment washed over her, but she kept her chin high. "You spoke a woman's name with such pain, I thought she had to be a lost love. And then when you said freeing *our* slaves, I assumed she must have been your wife."

"Yet you never thought to simply ask?"

"I thought it too painful for you."

Those expressive eyes bore into hers, then he turned back to the yard, where the water looked like ink flowing from a giant's overturned ink bottle. The shadows clung to the trees, settling the house into darkness.

Had she angered him? Did he think....No. She would not assume. "Have I upset you?"

"No. I am merely thinking."

"About?"

"You."

He said no more, and her stomach churned. Why must she be filled with this tumult of unfamiliar emotions? Is this what Ella meant when she'd mentioned matters of the heart could be complicated...and painful? Love seemed to be nothing like what happened in books. No, life was far too messy for that.

But this ache she felt, it couldn't be love. She glanced at Tristan, noting the hard set to his jaw, and decided that no, what she'd felt had been compassion for his condition and sorrow for his pain. She'd merely taken her own loneliness and conjured up a story to ease its sting.

Suddenly, he whirled around and grabbed her shoulders, and she let out a startled yelp. His eyes widened, but he didn't release her.

"Marry me."

She blinked. Surely he jested! "What?"

"Marry me, Opal, please."

Opal stared at him, the pain in his eyes reflecting something in her own heart. She looked at him for what felt like an eternity, and then shook her head. "But I don't love you."

Her words seared through his chest, burning in a way he never knew words could. She looked up at him, tears in her eyes, and he realized his mistake. He ran into this as though it had been a battle, and she a contested field to be won. He'd given no thought to the gentle ways that women wanted.

Tristan gently brushed his fingers down her jaw. "Marry me, and you will."

She gasped, her eyes flying wide. "I...." Tears welled and she spun away, pulling from his grasp.

He let her go, and watched her run inside, berating his own idiocy. What right did he have to say such a thing? He could not *make* her love him.

Tristan waited for several moments, until he was sure she had escaped him, and then went into the house. Mrs. Martin had given him a guest chamber above stairs, a sparse area with a straw tick and a washbasin, but he dared not go up there tonight.

He found the oil lantern in the parlor and lit it, turning the wick down low. He located the book he sought on the shelf near the fireplace and opened the thick volume in his lap. Where to begin?

Where would he find verses that would teach him

how to conquer his tongue? To speak with gentleness, to love another? Who would show him how to erase the darkness that still tried to cling to his soul?

He flipped the pages, and decided to start with the gospels.

Opal tossed in her bed, unable to sleep. In one day, *two* men had declared to marry her. And here she'd thought she might very well end up an old maid. She stuck her head under her pillow. Neither had been what she wanted.

I don't love you.

She groaned, burying her face.

Marry me, and you will.

Despite it all, despite logic and reality, she had always dreamed of something more. Something akin to what Ella and Westley shared. She wanted a man to look at her like that, to sweep her into his arms and declare his love for her.

Instead, she had a foul man who aimed to do nothing but use her and another who…well, what *did* Tristan want? He'd blurted a marriage proposal out of nowhere, right on the heels of telling her what had happened to his sister. And he'd claimed that all she had to do was speak vows, and love would come. She might be inexperienced, but even she didn't believe such a thing to be true.

Her stomach twisted. What a fool she'd been to assume. Of course he would have that much pain over the evils done to his sister. What was wrong with her to think any affection a man showed must be of a romantic nature?

Opal groaned and tossed again, and her mattress sank. She'd forgotten to tighten the ropes. Not that it mattered, as she doubted she could get comfortable anyway.

Finally, she willed her racing mind to still, snuggled down in the depression in the center of her bed, and started to pray.

Chapter Twelve

Two days had passed. Two days of watching the waters leave debris, scrubbing the mud clinging to the house, and thanking Tristan for slogging to the kitchen to bring back what little was to be had from their mostly ruined stores.

For two days Opal had thrown herself into the work of cleaning and avoiding speaking to Tristan of anything more than the most basic necessities. To his credit he didn't pressure her, only watched her with those eyes that always said too much.

She'd come to a clear conclusion. Obviously, he'd offered to marry her to save her from the devices of Mr. Weir. Well, she appreciated the sentiment, but she would not be a bride of obligation nor sacrifice, no matter how noble the intentions. That carpetbagger could not force her to wed, and she would not be caught off guard again.

The dog began barking, and her heart leapt into her throat. Had thinking of the scoundrel hastened his return? She dropped the cleaning rag from her hand and darted to the door, needing to check again that it remained locked. But when she reached the door, it was not a fancy blue chaise that churned up the mud, but a pair of sturdy, if mismatched, geldings, and the Remington carriage.

Opal flung open the door, her heart thudding against her ribs. Westley Remington swung down out of the seat, his boots sucking in the ankle-deep leavings of the river. He lifted Ella down next, her weight seeming nothing to him. Ella pulled her simple skirts above the muck, revealing sturdy boots that laced up past her ankles.

Ella's eyes found Opal's, and she burst into a smile. Mr. Remington gave a wave, and the two made their way onto the porch.

"Oh," Ella said, "I was worried I would find only a foundation left when I finally arrived!" She grabbed Opal and pulled her into a hug. "I came as soon as we could get down the road." She cast her husband a seething glance. "I would have walked here yesterday, if he would have let me."

Opal settled into her friend's embrace, unable to keep her smile contained.

"Indeed," Mr. Remington said, ignoring his wife's retort. "I am surprised you fared this well. Did the water come inside?"

She pulled free of Ella's arms and turned to him. "No, thankfully it did not rise above the back porch. It flooded the kitchen, the barn, and the smokehouse, but the main house is unharmed."

He nodded, his thick, dark hair caressing his forehead. "A blessing."

"Aye," Ella agreed. "And a blessing you are safe.

How is your mother?"

Opal gestured to the door. "She is a bit flustered over all of the excitement, but doing as well as can be expected."

At Opal's urging, the Remingtons passed into the house and headed to the parlor. She made sure to secure the door, having to nudge Shadow back—lest he think to come in the house—and then moved to join them.

She hesitated in the doorway, willing her emotions to calm. Ella, it seemed, would not be fooled by such a tactic. No sooner had she settled on the settee than she rose from it again.

"What's wrong?" She hurried to grasp Opal's hands.

"A great deal is wrong," Mama said from behind.

Opal tried not to groan, but Ella narrowed her eyes as the sound escaped unbidden from Opal's throat. Couldn't they just enjoy friendly company for a *few* moments before divesting the tale?

Mama swept past them into the parlor, not bothering to spare Opal a glance. "Come. There is much to tell."

Opal glanced around the foyer and hall for Tristan, but saw no sign of him. Better he be somewhere occupying himself anyway. She hadn't given the grisly details of what had happened with Mr. Weir prior to their bout with the river, and she didn't really want him overly informed.

Besides, Ella would probably want to ask him far too many questions. Opal sat next to Ella and listened to Mama recount all that had occurred, surprised at how candid she relayed it. Opal watched her, marveling at how the past days' events seemed to have changed Mama. She looked tired, but she also seemed more genuine than she normally appeared with company. Not to mention more animated.

Mama left out no details, and at several intervals had to pause to answer Mr. Remington's heated questions. By the end of it, Ella was grasping Opal's hand so tightly it started to hurt.

"Make no mistake, Mrs. Martin," Mr. Remington said, his expression stony. "I will see that scoundrel banned from these lands and run out of this town." He looked to Opal, and she wondered if such an expression was one a brother wore. "I will let no harm come to you, I promise."

The promise warmed her, and she was thankful for friends who were truly more like family.

"Tristan asked me to marry him," Opal blurted.

Silence settled on the room, and she lowered her eyes.

"You did not tell me," Mama said. "I thought he had been too busy with the chores to have the opportunity."

Opal's eyes flew wide. "You knew?"

Mama gave a satisfied smile. "Of course, child." Then she frowned. "You did not accept?"

A shout arose from outside, cutting off her answer. They hurried to the window, but Mr. Remington reached it before she did, and his figure blocked her view. He made a funny noise that reminded her of one of Shadow's growls, and then darted out of the parlor.

The women followed on his heels and piled out onto the front porch. Another shout arose, joined by the feverish barking of Tristan's dog. She craned her neck, trying to look around Mr. Remington's large frame as he hastened to the front stairs. A flash of movement grabbed her attention, and she stepped around Mama to see. Two figures rolled out from behind the Remington carriage, spraying mud.

Opal let out a squeal. Mr. Weir had returned! His horse sidestepped and whinnied, hooves flying dangerously close to the struggling men. Tristan shouted something, and then flipped Mr. Weir onto his back, pinning him in the muck.

"Stay here," Mr. Remington commanded as he nearly leapt off the second step. He acted as though he were still an officer in the Federal Army and the women were his troops!

The ladies looked at one another, and Ella seemed to share Opal's thoughts. They both hefted their skirts and scurried down the front steps. Mr. Remington called for the men to halt, but Tristan had Mr. Weir's shirt collar in his hands and was saying something Opal couldn't hear.

Ella grabbed her arm and pulled them to a stop next to the carriage, just a few paces from the men. "Not too close. I've seen enough fighting men to know you never place yourself within reach."

Opal frowned and made a move to step forward, but Ella held firm.

"They won't mean for you to get hurt, but when their fists are flying, they don't seem to have much control over where blows land."

She sounded so earnest that Opal relented. The shouts stopped, drawing her eyes back to the men whose suits were covered in thick river sediment.

Mr. Remington clasped Tristan on his shoulder. "Rise, Mr. Stuart, and let us have words with this fellow."

Tristan sneered at Mr. Weir, and Opal couldn't help the kernel of satisfaction that blossomed over the look of fear covering his face. She crossed her arms. There. Let him see what it felt like.

Mr. Weir's eyes found hers, and narrowed. Tristan caught the expression and whirled around, seeing her.

"Opal," Tristan barked. "Return to the porch."

So now he thought to command her as well? She lifted her chin. "I will not. As this matter concerns me and my home, I shall stay."

Tristan opened his mouth as though to contest her, but then a spark flashed in his eyes and, to her great surprise, he grinned. "You are correct, Miss Martin. My apologies."

Underneath Tristan's weight, Mr. Weir groaned.

Ella put her fingers to her mouth, but couldn't quite contain her smirk. Her husband merely shook his head and turned his attention back to Mr. Weir. Tristan shoved off the man, earning another groan, and then stood back to watch him slowly gain his feet.

Mr. Weir brushed himself off, glaring at Tristan. "What is the meaning of this? I will have the law after you, vagrant, for attacking me without cause!"

Tristan's fingers flexed at his sides. "Without

cause?" He looked at Mr. Remington. "I would say attempting to threaten a lady into a betrothal in order to steal her home is an adequate cause. Would you not agree, sir?"

Opal pressed her lips together. What all had Mama shared with him? Opal had given him no details.

Mr. Remington nodded. "I say that is fair and just cause indeed." He turned his palms out. "But if you wish, Mr. Weir, I will accompany you to town to speak with the Federal officials. I know them all quite well."

Mr. Weir blanched, then balled his fists. "The lady agreed to marry me." His voice seemed less forceful than before. He glanced at Opal again. "There is no crime here."

Tristan made a rumbling noise and took a step closer, causing Mr. Weir to lean back and begin sputtering. Shadow seemed to take this as an invitation to renew his barking. The dog bounced around the men, letting his canine dissatisfaction with the situation be known, and earning a worried stare from the carpetbagger. Opal had never liked the creature more.

Tristan merely held out his hand toward the dog, and the canine quieted. Shadow sat back on his haunches, his eyes riveted on Mr. Weir.

"As the lady is present..." Tristan gestured to Opal. "We shall merely ask her."

She swallowed, annoyed with her pounding pulse. With Tristan here to protect her, she should not feel afraid. His warm eyes offered encouragement, and her resolve strengthened.

Opal tore her eyes away from Tristan and let her

gaze rest on Mr. Weir's red face. "I do not wish to marry you."

"But, you said—"

She squared her shoulders, finding more confidence. "I merely said what I had to say in order to get you to leave. Surely after the way you treated us, and the unholy insinuations you made, you cannot expect for me to want to marry you."

Mr. Weir sneered, once more revealing the man she had seen in the house. Instinctively, she took a step back, and Ella held her arm for support.

Tristan stepped between them, his voice dangerously low. "There you have it. She has no desire to wed you or further suffer your intentions. You will remove yourself from this land and never return."

"But, I—"

Tristan snagged the front of his shirt. "Are we clear?"

Mr. Weir glowered, and Mr. Remington stepped closer. Tristan released him and moved back, wiping his hands on his trousers.

Finally, Mr. Weir flung his hands up. "Fine! This place is a ramshackle heap anyway." He bared his teeth at Opal. "Not to mention the fact that she would be far too much work to refine and not nearly pretty enough to be worth the trouble." He made a rude gesture at Tristan and then grabbed the pommel of his horse's saddle. "I will take my money elsewhere."

Tristan tossed him the horse's reins. "See that you do."

Without casting her another look, Mr. Weir

grabbed the reins and yanked the horse's head to the side. The frightened creature let out a startled whinny, then churned up the muddy grass in her yard as it lurched away.

In another moment, the horse was galloping down the drive, leaving Opal with a profound sense of relief.

Chapter Thirteen

Tristan stood heaving, watching the scoundrel disappear down the drive. A strong hand clapped him on the back.

"I daresay that fellow won't be bothering us again."

Tristan turned to the stranger. "I hope not." He glanced at Opal. She and her friend, this man's wife, chatted softly with their heads together.

The dark-haired man followed his gaze. "My wife is rather fond of Miss Martin."

Tristan nodded absently, unable to tear his gaze from her face.

"I'm Westley Remington," he said, giving Tristan's shoulder a friendly squeeze. "And you must be Mr. Tristan Stuart."

"What?" Tristan turned. "Oh, yes, of course." He stuck his hand out. "A pleasure, Mr. Remington."

The man gave his hand a firm shake. He glanced at the women and then back to Tristan. "You have my word no harm will come to Miss Martin so long as I am near."

Tristan nodded again, but felt the strangest irritation at the words. Almost as though he believed *he* should be the one pledging to protect her. But she had refused him.

Love is patient, love is kind...love is a sacrifice, and it is a choice. It is not a mere feeling.

Words from long ago surfaced, and he remembered the day he'd heard them. He'd been twenty, just after Fort Sumter. He'd been restlessly sitting in chapel, his father and his older brothers only days from leaving to join their new units. The pastor had spoken of love for family and for country. Of how love meant you had to sacrifice and honor those you loved, and it wasn't merely a feeling.

His eyes followed Opal to the house. Could she love him in that way? She had already demonstrated those qualities in the many things she'd done for him. She'd even risked her life, jumping into the swirling river, when she thought she could save him. His throat constricted. She'd leapt for him, even though she couldn't swim.

Were such things not at least sparks of love?

Mr. Remington moved to follow, and Tristan gave Shadow a pat on the head and a command to stay and watch before shoving his hands into his pockets and making his way toward the house that looked so much like his own lost home.

But what was home, really? It wasn't the brick and mortar, but the people embraced within. And heaven help him, if home was a place that held the heart, then his heart had just stepped inside a place called Riverbend.

Tristan lingered with Mr. Remington on the porch

after the women slipped inside. The other man stood silently for a time, looking out over the yard. It still bore the signs of the flood, but Tristan had removed the majority of the fallen limbs and debris.

Tristan shifted his feet, feeling an odd compulsion to bare his battered thoughts to this stranger. "She refused my proposal of marriage."

"Did she?" Mr. Remington cocked his head. "Are you sure?"

He scowled. Did the man think him daft? How would he not know if she had refused such a request? Still, he sifted through the conversation and examined the memory. "Well, she said she didn't love me, and then ran away." He lifted his hands. "I think it is safe to assume her answer is no."

"Ah, well," Mr. Remington said, rocking back on his heels. "One thing I have learned about women is that you can never make assumptions about their intentions."

As Opal had made assumptions about Millie? He thought back, remembering the emotions that had played across her features. Yes, now that he thought on it, he was sure the look in her eyes had not only been sorrow for the story he'd shared, but also a different hurt. A pain of her own.

He looked at Mr. Remington—and oddly, the fellow smiled.

Why would Opal look that way? Unless... He glanced at the house, where the door stood ajar. Unless she thought Tristan yet loved another, and the idea pained her? "She distinctly said she did not love me."

But if she truly did not love him, then why be upset over thinking he yearned for a lost love?

"Hmm." Mr. Remington glanced at the door. "When we were first together, I found it frustrating when Ella would lob hurtful words at me, even when I could clearly see she scarcely believed them."

Tristan stared at him. That hardly sounded like the fairy tale love he'd expected, given Opal's doe-eyed recount of the tale.

"It wasn't until later," Remington continued, "that I realized she said things as a way of building walls against me, in order to protect herself. It wasn't until I had the courage to scale those walls that I truly understood her."

The man spoke in riddles.

"Perhaps," he said with a sly smile, "you might find another opportunity to discuss things with her."

"Perhaps. Though I doubt she will welcome the conversation."

"Then maybe it's time to declare your feelings."

Tristan eyed the man a moment, his blood heating. "Yes, I suppose you are right." How could he expect to win her, if he wasn't willing to fight for her?

As Mr. Weir galloped off, Ella grasped her arm so tightly that Opal winced. "Opal Martin, what's wrong with you?"

Opal felt her jaw unhinge and snapped it closed. "What?" Should she not feel elation watching that greedy lowlife run away like a dog with its tail between its legs?

"Not that," Ella whispered, ducking her head near Opal's so Tristan and Westley wouldn't overhear. "I mean *him*."

"Tristan?" She glanced at him, noting the satisfied set to his shoulders.

Ella tugged on her and they started back toward the house. "Yes, of course. Who else?"

Opal frowned, and simply let Ella lead her away. She loved her friend, but the lady did have a knack for the dramatic. They made their way across the wet ground, trying to avoid the worst of the mud.

Mama stood on the porch like a queen overlooking her subjects, her smile radiant. Though Opal couldn't help but wonder why she seemed so jovial for someone who had just lost her opportunity to move to Massachusetts. They'd never have the money now. The thought brought both relief and guilt. She shouldn't be so selfish. Mama watched them approach, then followed them inside, leaving the door ajar for the men.

Opal tugged her arm away from her friend and paused in the foyer. "Thank heavens that scoundrel is gone. Be sure to extend my heartfelt thanks to your husband."

Mama made a scoffing noise, but Opal ignored her.

Ella lifted her eyebrows, two slashes of vibrant red across her pale features. "Aye, now, you know I will, but I daresay there's another fellow who deserves the bulk of your gratitude." Her accent always became more pronounced when she was excited over something.

"Yes, of course. I will thank Tristan as well, as that would only be proper." Opal kept her shoulders straight, and her tone properly controlled. No one needed to know how it had thrilled her to see him fighting for her freedom from that awful man. They would deem such a thing silly.

Ella rolled her eyes. "For the most romantically inclined young woman I have ever known, you certainly missed the rather romantic nature of a dashing gentleman coming to your rescue."

Something burned in the back of her throat and she swallowed it down. "Life is not like fairy tales or romance novels. I know that now."

Mama wrapped her arm around Opal's shoulders and drew her close. "Oh, my sweet girl, I am sorry I criticized you for reading and for not treasuring your tender heart. I do not wish for you to become cynical." Her voice hitched. "And certainly not on account of my bitterness."

The tears that gathered in the back of her eyes wet her lashes.

"No, life is not like a story," Mama continued, "where every problem is immediately resolved and every couple falls in love and then never has a care in the world." She put both hands on Opal's shoulders and looked at her intently. "But *real* love is much better. You are stronger for the pain you fight through together, and closer for the wounds you help one another heal. Love isn't without conflict, nor is it without sacrifice. But, my darling, *that* is the love that seeps all the way into our souls and has the substance to last."

Ella sniffled. "Your mother is very wise. Do not think that Westley swooped in and, from the moment I saw him, I knew we would be together. Our love was forged through hardship and is still growing. I love him more now than I ever did, and I believe with careful tending, that love will continue to strengthen."

Opal blinked away the tears. "So love is not just a rampant attraction and a wool-headed feeling?" She said it only half in jest.

Ella laughed. "No, I daresay at times it is best described as a most frustrating and persistent devotion to tend to another's well-being." She grinned. "There are times you feel weightless and fluttery, but more often it is the comforting, steady feeling of a solid bond."

"So this thing…" Opal said, glancing at the two women in front of her in turn, "this thing that I feel that has me yearning to care for him, to make his hurts lessen and his smile come more often, could that be love?"

Mama squeezed her shoulders. "It is how I started with your father, and it bloomed into something much more."

The door creaked open, and the object of their discussion poked his head through the door. Concern lit in his eyes, those great pools of emotion that swept her away. "Are you well?"

She stepped forward and nodded. "I am." She glanced at Mama, who gave her a nod. "May we speak in the parlor?"

He seemed surprised. "I came hoping to do just that."

The others dismissed themselves to join Mr. Remington on the porch, and Opal nervously followed Tristan into the parlor where he took a seat on the settee.

She hesitated only a moment, and then settled next to him. "Thank you for protecting me and my home. You didn't have to do that."

He reached over and took both of her hands in his calloused ones. "If you would let me, I would spend my life protecting you from every hurt I could."

She opened her mouth, but he released her hands to put his thumb over her lips.

"Please, I must say this now, while I still have the courage to do so."

Opal nodded against the warmth of his palm pressed against her cheek.

"I am broken and scarred, Opal. War has made me a haunted man. Shadows cling to my dreams, and battle still haunts my thoughts. I have no illusions about being the man you deserve, but I know that when I am with you, I want to be a better man. I want to learn to let God grow me into someone who can love you in all the ways you deserve."

She shuddered under the sincerity in his eyes.

He let them drift closed and rested his forehead against hers. His tender words brushed against her heart like a feather. "If you would have me, I would like to take this seed of love and nurture it." He leaned back, and his face filled her vision. "Marry me, and if you have a mustard seed's worth of love for me as well, perhaps we can grow it into a great and mighty tree that will harbor us from life's storms."

She slipped her fingers up into the tangle of his hair, caked with mud from his encounter with Mr. Weir. "Oh, Tristan. I offer you a timid heart and, with it, hope to help you bind wounds and encourage you. I would like to grow this seed of love with you and see where it takes us."

He sighed, and slipped his hand up to the back of her head. When his lips caressed hers, something in her soared, and she pressed closer. And in one intoxicating moment, she found that feeling she'd only ever read about.

Chapter Fourteen

Riverbend Plantation
November 1865

Mama crossed her arms and eyed the table. "It is a Yankee holiday, you know that, don't you?"

Ella laughed. "Mr. Lincoln declared it a day of giving thanks unto the Lord. I say that supersedes old war alliances." She winked at Mama. "And besides, with the army bringing in extra supplies to ensure we don't forget to feast, it works into our plans marvelously."

Opal frowned. What did that mean?

Sibby burst into the dining room, carrying a tray laden with an entire baked ham. Opal's eyes widened. "Wherever did you get *that*?"

The woman set the platter down and waved a hand at her. "Never you mind 'bout that." She eyed Opal's gown, still covered with a stained apron from where she'd been helping in the kitchen. "Don't you think it's time you done went and got ready?"

"Yes, it is," Ella said, grasping Opal's hand and giving it a tug. "Come. I have a surprise for you."

Opal shook her head as Basil came in with another

armful of food. Where had they gotten such abundance? She hated to see all that go to waste, as it would surely take them a week to eat it all. They would fare better forgetting this silly day of feasting and store that food up for the winter.

She allowed Ella to take her upstairs to her room, keeping her misgivings to herself. Tristan had been rather excited about everyone coming together to have this feast, and she would not spoil it for him.

As the weeks had passed and they had spent more time in one another's company, the seed she had first felt had, indeed, begun to grow. She and Tristan planned to marry come spring. In the meantime, he had taken up residence with the Remingtons, though he came to Riverbend every day, slowly restoring her home back into good repair.

Ella strutted into Opal's bedchamber and flung open her wardrobe. She reached inside and pulled out a great heap of shiny purple fabric.

Opal stared at it a moment, and then pressed her lips together. "I hate to say it, Ella, but I fear that color will not look good on you. It…" She shrugged. "It doesn't complement your hair."

"You silly girl!" Ella laughed, pulling her into a hug and crumpling the massive gown between them. "It's for you! Sibby and I started working on it the very day you first told me about Mr. Stuart."

"You did?"

Ella held the gown up to Opal's shoulders. "Indeed. And this will look splendid on you."

Opal looked down at the shimmering fabric. "It's a

ball gown."

Ella giggled again. "And therefore perfect for to-night's ball."

"What?"

She received only another laugh at her confusion, and Ella would only reveal that it had been Tristan's idea. As Opal pulled the gown over her head, she decided to quit asking questions and merely enjoy the frippery.

For at least the next hour Ella fussed over her until Opal felt like she might unravel from all the attention. Her hair alone seemed to require an eternity's worth of tugging, combing, and pinning. Finally, Ella stepped back and declared her finished. They went across the hall to Mama's chamber, where Opal could see herself in the full-length mirror.

She gasped. What happened to the scrawny girl in a ragged yellow dress? Here instead stood a woman in a resplendent ball gown that shimmered in the light. Perfectly crafted and forming to every curve, each ruffle, pleat, and button made a stroke of a masterpiece. Her eyes welled.

"No, don't you cry." Ella squeezed her hand. "We don't want your eyes puffy."

"Oh!" Mama's voice came from the door. "She is a vision!"

Mama's own eyes welled, threatening to cause the moisture to escape from Opal's eyes as well. "Isn't it beautiful, Mama? Ella made it for me." She looked back at her friend. "She says we are having a ball…?"

Mama clasped her hands. "Indeed, we are! A feast

and a ball the likes of which this old house hasn't seen in years!"

She seemed so excited that Opal didn't dare comment on the unnecessary extravagance.

"And," Mama continued, "It will be a grand bit of fun before I go to Massachusetts."

Opal stilled. "What are you talking about?"

"I am going to go and spend a few months with Eunice. It will be good for us both. We'll have Christmas, and the spring…" Mama smiled. "It will be good."

"You are…you're going to leave me here alone?"

Mama's eyes glistened. "Of course not, dear. You have Tristan to look out for you."

"But…"

"Enough." Mama waved her hand and pointed Opal toward the stairs. "We'll talk more about it after the feast."

"Yes," Ella said. "It's time we go. You can talk of these things later."

Opal thought to protest, but instead she followed the two oddly sniffling women downstairs. Evening had begun to fall upon them, cloaking the house in rose-hued light.

Laughter came from the parlor, filling the air and washing the quiet walls of Riverbend in sparkling anticipation. Flickering light shimmered along the floor, creating gilded patterns on the polished wood. She glanced to Mama for explanation, but Mama only smiled. They paused in the foyer, and Ella pulled Opal into an embrace. Then she slipped into the parlor, and soft music began to play.

Mama took hold of Opal's arm, and guided her inside.

Her breath caught. From every surface in the parlor, tiny flames danced atop a multitude of candles, casting the room in a golden glow. She put her fingers to her lips. Not only were the Remingtons and their household here, but at least twenty of her neighbors filled both the gentlemen's and ladies' parlors. The massive doors between them had been pulled wide, joining the two spaces as they had not been since Daddy left for war. The people, dressed in their finest, smiled and whispered, all staring at her.

Her feet slowed. "Mama, what's happening?"

Mama patted her hand. Somewhere in the corner, a man played a sweet song from a fiddle, and the music began to swell. The group parted, and there at the far end of the parlors stood Tristan.

Dressed in his uniform, he stood tall and proud, a reminder of the soldier he had been. His hair had been neatly combed, and he clasped his hands behind his back. When their eyes met, he smiled. The light of his smile shone through his eyes, even at this distance.

Next to him stood Reverend Carlson, his back to the hearth where Daddy had often enjoyed his pipe. Opal's eyes widened and she looked back to Tristan, who now grinned broadly.

Mama squeezed her arm. "Go now, darling. He waits for you."

The room seemed to stand still, even as the music whirled and the candles twinkled. Tristan held her gaze, keeping her steady as she passed applauding neighbors to stand next to him in front of the reverend.

Tristan took her hand and placed it to his lips, his eyes mischievous. "Surprised, my love?"

"Yes," she whispered, trying to hold back a laugh. "I never knew a bride could be surprised by her own wedding." She glanced over the gathered crowd. "I thought we were to wait until spring?"

"And I thought I would try for a grand surprise instead." A hint of worry entered his eyes. "You don't like it?"

"Oh, Tristan." She stepped closer to him, ignoring the gasps of the crowd. "It is the most romantic thing I've ever seen."

He cupped her face and lowered his forehead to hers. "I love you, Opal."

"And I you."

When his lips touched hers, the preacher sputtered something about how that was supposed to come after the vows. But Opal didn't care. She let her lips linger on his for a moment longer.

When he pulled his head back, his eyes had darkened, but for a different reason. On this day, they were filled with more light than shadows. And she prayed that as their days passed, together they would grow a love that would help them weather all of life's sorrows and further erase the clinging stain of war.

As her own love reflected in the face of the man across from her, those roots took hold deep in her heart, binding her to him.

Tristan grabbed her hands again as the crowd laughed and the good reverend gave him a scowl.

Reverend Carlson cleared his throat. "Shall we start over? From the beginning this time?"

Tristan laughed. "Yes, but make it quick." He gave her a roguish wink. "For it's time our fairy tale began."

Dear reader,

"But I don't love you."
"Marry me, and you will."

Those were the words spoken by my grandparents more than sixty-five years ago. It was the winter of 1951, he was in the Air Force and had taken her on a grand total of three dates. Certain he didn't want to return to duty without her by his side, my grandfather proposed to my grandmother, and she accepted his claim. They married right away. Their love bloomed into four children, four granddaughters, and ten great-grandchildren.

I've always loved that story and wanted to someday put it in one of my books. It just seemed to fit in Opal and Tristan's tale. I hope it stirred you the way it did me. If you wouldn't mind taking a few moments to leave a review online, I would really appreciate it. It only takes a sentence or two and means so much.

If you haven't already read all about Ella and Westley, you can find their full story in *In His Eyes*.

Visit me at www.StepheniaMcGee.com for books and news, and be sure to join my newsletter to be the first to hear about new covers and releases, be part of subscriber-only giveaways, and more!

Happy reading!
Stephenia

Made in the USA
Monee, IL
10 June 2023